Unchain Me

C.A. Grieco

Copyright © 2024 by C.A. Grieco

All rights reserved.

No portion of this book may be reproduced in any form without written permission from the publisher or author, except as permitted by U.S. copyright law.

This book is dedicated to every single one of you.
Whatever battle you've fought or are still fighting,
never forget that you are not alone;
you are strong, and you are worthy.

Please note there are triggers in this book
Domestic Violence
Murder
Pregnancy
Pre-term Labor
NICU stay
Cancer
Cancer treatments/ side effects

Chapter One

TRISH

It's been six months since I almost died.

Six months since I laid in a puddle of blood on our cold kitchen tile while the black edges closed in as the man I thought loved me walked away.

Six months since that eerie peace settled in, and I accepted I would never wake up again.

Yet here I lay next to the monster himself as he sleeps peacefully. His blonde strands of hair wisp softly across his forehead. For a moment, it's easy to see the man I fell desperately in love with and not the one that shoved me on to the vase he'd smashed in a fit of rage. The man that stared at me with disgust painting his features as I begged for help.

Right now, he isn't that man. He is just Brett, the man I trusted with everything. The man I planned my future with. Wanted to marry. Start a family with.

I can't be that woman, though. I know how easy it is to get wrapped in the apologies. I've held my best friend, Claire, in my arms many nights when the nightmares of her dad taking her mom's life became too much.

Her mom stayed, and paid a price I refuse to pay.

For months I've watched him play *boyfriend of the year*, while pretending I'd brushed it all under the rug. Waiting for the perfect moment to leave as filled suitcases sat dust covered in our storage closet.

The moment has come in the worst way. My best friend losing her younger brother and taking a job halfway across the country. Claire only lives a half hour from me. There was a time when we wouldn't let a week pass without spending a day together. Her brother's spiraling was the perfect excuse for me to pull away and hide the fact that my dream life had exploded into a mess I could no longer clean up.

Brett doesn't know Michael died. I know I should have run to Claire the moment it happened and helped her plan his funeral. That's what someone that's been your friend most of your life does when you lose the only family you have left.

Instead, I've pretended nothing has changed while I meticulously planned my freedom. He has no clue he will wake up tomorrow without me by his side. I'm not sure if he will even bother trying to find me. If he does, the first place he will go is Claire's house. But we'll be long gone by then.

The thought of constantly looking over my shoulder eats at me. I know fear can do weird things to people, and I fear I may truly never know peace again. But I shove those thoughts away. For now, I can only focus on escaping this nightmare.

I ask myself every day why I haven't just called the police. Yet as I stare at the man in front of me, I can't imagine locking him away. I know how pathetic that sounds. The visions of the good moments dance behind my eyes. The man he used to be. Part of me can't accept that he doesn't really exist.

I pull myself from the warmth of the blankets. Every movement feels like it drags as I watch the even rise and fall of his chest, just waiting for his eyes to pop open and my entire plan to be ruined. Somehow, I make it to the standing position without him noticing. Tip-toeing across the room, I grab my phone from the nightstand. There is a brand new one in the suitcase downstairs. I already texted anyone that mattered the new number, but I know better than to leave anything behind that could somehow lead him to me.

I look back as I get to the door. Part of me glued in place. The pain of leaving behind every plan, dream, and hope for my future splinters throughout me. I push myself forward, snapping the last threads that desperately want to forgive him. Even though my footsteps are near silent, I can't help but cringe at every one of them. Staring over my shoulder the entire way down the steps, I grab three of the four oversized suitcases, realizing the last one is too much to carry in one trip. I have no time to check what's packed inside of it. I just hope it's nothing important before I walk out the front door. Years of memories I couldn't pack without him noticing are left scattered throughout the house.

The warm summer night air hits me as I open the door. Looking around, I spot the Uber a block over where I told him to park. Realizing it took me longer to get out of the house than I had planned, I take off running towards it. Thankfully, the driver sees me and climbs out of his seat, popping the trunk. I quickly toss my bags inside, still glancing over my shoulder.

"Ma'am, are you okay?" The driver asks me as he closes the trunk, concern coating his words.

I finally take the time to look at him. He is an older man, probably in his seventies. His gray hair is combed nicely to one side. His eyes are locked in on the empty sidewalk behind us as he tries to see what my paranoia has me searching for.

"I'm so sorry about that. I'm fine," I say, sliding my mask in place and shooting him a smile.

He looks unconvinced but opens my door and allows me to slide in. I look back down the empty sidewalk out of instinct as a shuddering breath escapes me. The poor old man's eyes follow again before he quickly shuts my door and practically runs to his side, not even bothering with his seat belt before taking off. I make a mental note to give him five stars for dealing with my chaos.

"I can call the police if you're in some kind of trouble," he says cautiously about ten minutes later, looking me over in the rearview mirror.

"I appreciate it, but I really am okay," I reassure him. "Could you stop up here by the river really quickly?"

He nods, driving a bit further before pulling over to the side of the near desolate city streets. I step out, looking across the Hudson. Climbing up to the ledge, I let the cool breeze embrace me as I hurl the phone as far as I can manage, watching it disappear into the darkness.

"This is the right choice," I whisper to myself, staring out.

"Ma'am, please come down from there." I look back at the panicked face of the driver behind me as he hesitates to move towards me.

I climb down, realizing how it must look to him before getting back into the car as I watch his shoulders visibly relax. Maybe I should explain myself, but I don't have the energy. I collapse against the cool window of the car as the adrenaline high finally fades and exhaustion hits me.

Right now, I just need to get to the only other person I've ever trusted. I know she is so drowned in her own hell she won't see me breaking. And that's exactly what I need. She won't pick me apart until I tell her the truth. A truth I know I don't have in me to share with anyone yet. Tomorrow we will bury her brother, then we are heading halfway across the country. Once things settle down, I will tell her everything. As the distance from the house grows, comfort fills me for the first time in years.

Chapter Two

TRISH

Two months later

The sky behind my laptop screen changes to different colors of oranges and pink as the warm early-August air wraps around me. I stare out, taking a moment to let the beauty of it all sink in. I never had time to do this back at home. Not that it would have mattered. The sky was nothing but buildings and smog in the city.

At the time, I embraced it. The constant hustle of the world around me was something I used to thrive on.

The first day we moved here, I walked out and sat exactly where I am now. The sun was just rising on the horizon, and I had never seen anything like it. My mind was completely silent. The chaos of the city made it easy to drown out the world. Here you have no choice but to see its beauty. You can actually breathe. I watch as the sun brightens the endless fields before me. The tractors sit quietly amongst the endless plowed lines. The fields seeming to come to life as the workers move throughout the scene.

Last night plays over in my head. I was the worst friend. I ended up yelling at Claire when she saw the scar across my back—the one I've so desperately tried to hide from her. I should have just finally been honest. She was trying to help me, and I said things I'm not sure how to take back. I keep pushing her further away when the truth is I just want to protect her from carrying even more emotional weight than she already does. As I look around at the endlessness surrounding me, I feel truly alone. It seems like no matter how much I try to tell myself to stop, I am spiraling further into the mess.

I want nothing more than to stare out in peace and pretend there isn't an entire world I need to face, but I have to figure out how my client's account is getting hacked. This is the third security breach in a month. It's something that hasn't happened in the last five years I have been handling their file. Thankfully, they haven't taken anything of great importance, but my client is losing faith in me. I know it's completely my fault; I've been so caught up in my life crumbling around me I've been missing things I normally wouldn't. Losing them would be a nightmare since they are not only my biggest client, they're also my biggest referral source.

It's driving me crazy. I've worked so hard to get where I am. As a woman in any IT field, I already feel like I'm not given as many chances as my male counterparts. That's why I started my business five years ago with only a hope I could build a life for myself. Normally, I'm damn good at what I do. I can't tell you how many times other people would come to me for help with an issue. Even when I would solve the problem, they would still take the bigger clients over me. I was in complete shock when *B & N Enterprises* followed me out the door. Apparently, when they heard I was leaving to start my firm, they didn't think twice about giving me a shot.

Now here I am, blowing it. I want to scream at how unfair it all is. I can't afford to lose anything else.

Just another piece of my perfectly constructed life that is crumbling beneath me. I wonder how much can break before I can no longer hold it together? How long can I pretend that this façade I put on isn't all for show?

I know I'm lying to myself. I've already started to show the cracks. No matter how hard I fight, the pieces keep splintering out and they are hurting the one person I love the most. The person I'm trying like hell to protect. I hear her shuffling inside the house behind me. My best friend in the entire world. The one that took me with her without a question, and has loved me through everything. She's getting ready for work, and I know her ride will be here soon.

My heart begs me to go talk to her. I spent the entire night listening to her cry. I walked to her door and almost knocked but decided against it. I am so afraid that if I tell her all of my secrets, she will bury herself in my pain like she did with her brother, Michael. Claire will stop at nothing to save the people she loves. Even if that means drowning herself. The pain of knowing I'm wrong rips through me, but I can't tell her the truth. It might slice through the few strands she has left holding her together. I can't be weak. I did that once, and it damn near broke me. Right now, I have to focus... I can't lose this client.

My growling stomach pulls me from my mental fog as I look out to see the sun high in the sky. It's hot now. I've had to be out here for hours, and I think I finally figured out a way to keep everything locked down. I quickly shoot them an email and close my laptop, stretching and feeling the tightness in my muscles from being locked in the same position for hours. I walk to the fridge and grab the leftovers from the night before. It's just pasta since neither Claire nor I are master chefs, but we know our way around a can of sauce and box of noodles. It's showing in how my pants are fitting lately. It's far from a quick walk to an acai bowl around here.

I toss the noodles on the plate and chuck them in the microwave, ignoring how absolutely unappetizing they seem before going back to the fridge and pouring a glass of lemonade. The second the smell from the food hits me, I gag. My stomach turns and I all but throw the glass on the counter as I take off to the bathroom, throwing the lid open and crashing roughly to my knees before emptying the entire contents of my stomach into the toilet.

I can't stop. The smell somehow covers the house, filling the small bathroom with the offending odor. I can't get up to throw it away or even close the door. I puke up my guts until I'm left in a sweaty pile on the cool bathroom tile sweat dripping down me.

I pull myself up, walking to the microwave, holding my nose. I grab the disgusting dish, running out the door to the trash. As I throw open the door, I notice a large body in front of it. Arm raised as if he was just about to knock. I don't even take the time to look at him as I sprint past, leaving him standing there as I run to the trash and hold my breath as I open the lid and toss it inside.

A wave of dizziness hits me, and I try to balance myself.

When was the last time I ate something?

"Hey, why don't we get you sitting down somewhere."

In the chaos I completely forgot there was someone at the door watching this entire spectacle I am making. I look up, praying it's no one important, and I'm instead met with an extremely attractive man in a cowboy hat.

"Thank you, but I'm fine," I tell him, faking a smile.

"Okay," he says, looking unconvinced. "Well, could you humor me and let me at least follow you back to the house? It looks like you're about to fall over."

I want to argue that I will be fine, but part of me is scared I may not make it to the door. *Then what? I lay out in the heat and sweat to death because I'm stubborn?*

"Fine, thank you," I say, walking back to the front door.

My legs shake under me, but I fight past it. I can feel him behind me. Keeping far enough back that he isn't crowding me but also close enough that if I fell he'd have time to catch me. I thank God as my hand hits the doorknob.

"See? Totally fine," I say, twisting to face him as I step inside. As I do, that freaking smell hits me again. I don't have time to say another word as I puke down myself. It splatters the floor and across his boots.

Mortified doesn't even touch how I feel right now.

"I'm so sorry," I rush out as I turn to grab paper towels from the kitchen.

"Hey," he says, grabbing my shoulder to turn me towards him. "It's okay. Would you sit the hell down, though? You're going to pass out."

"I have to clean this up," I say, motioning to the mess.

"I'll clean it. Sit," he says, leaving no room for me to argue. I made a deal when I left New York I would never let a man tell me what to do again, but the way he says it is more concerned than angry, so I do what he says and I sit in the chair at the kitchen table as he pulls off his boots and puts them outside the door.

"Where are the paper towels?" he asks, while looking around the kitchen as if he owns it.

"Before you keep rummaging around, who are you?" I ask, realizing I've just welcomed a random man into my home to clean my vomit.

"Layton. I've been driving Claire to work since her car broke down. She forgot her notebook. I'm guessing you're Trish. Claire talks about you a lot," he says as he spots the paper towels on the counter and grabs them.

"Seriously, I will clean that. I feel bad enough I ruined your boots," I tell him, going to stand up.

"Would ya sit down? I work in cow shit for a living. Puke doesn't bother me. But you passing the hell out is somethin' I'd rather avoid." He wets a paper towel under the sink and brings it over to me. "Here, to wipe up."

"Thanks," I mumble.

"Do you have any cleaner?"

"Under the sink," I say, and he walks over to dig through the cleaning supplies we keep. He pulls out a couple bottles, reading the labels before seeming to be happy with one and standing up.

"I'm sorry about this. I just haven't been able to hold much down lately," I tell him honestly as I watch him scrub the puke from the ground. I fight myself not to go help him.

"I don't mind. I'm glad someone was here for you. You seriously should lie down. You still don't look great." He stands, throwing the paper towels away before taking the entire bag of trash and tying it up before walking it outside the door. "I'll grab that when I leave."

I stare at him in disbelief. In the last five minutes, I've seen this man do more than any man I have ever met in my life.

"Do you need a shower or something?" he asks, looking me up and down.

"I don't look great, and I need a shower? You don't hold back, do you?" I joke.

"Well, the puke-covered pale thing has me slightly overlooking the fact that you're hot as hell," he says, smiling. "Kinda worried about ya."

"I'll be okay," I say, feeling the blush heat my cheeks even though he just admitted I look gross. *He did also say I look hot.* "I just need to find something I can hold down. All I want is a bagel with cream cheese, so I'm sure I can figure out how to make that happen."

"Maybe some juice?" he asks, walking over to open the fridge which is completely empty. "How are you guys getting to the store?"

"We are trying to figure that part out."

"Why didn't Claire say anything?" he huffs out, going to open the cabinets again like he owns the place. "You guys have nothing."

"Technically, we have pasta and canned goods," I correct him.

He rolls his eyes. "I'm talking to Claire about this."

"No, she already feels horrible for making you drive her; she will never accept you taking her shopping. I told her I would figure it out. My plan was to ask Mrs. Mindy next door if I could go with her next week. She goes every other Tuesday."

"You're gonna starve to death by next Tuesday," he argues. "Tomorrow, be dressed at three. I'll come pick you up and we will run into town. You can tell Claire it was Mrs. Mindy."

"I can't do that. I don't even know you."

"Well, tomorrow I have to get groceries for my mom, so I'm going either way. Might as well tag along so you don't wither the hell away."

I want to argue with him, but he is right. I don't know if three cans of peas and a box of pasta are enough to keep us alive for an entire week.

"Fine," I huff. "Why do you even care?"

"I don't know," he says, rubbing a hand across his jaw. "That's just how it is out here. You help people that need a hand because one day it's gonna be your ass that needs the help. That's at least how I was raised,"

"I like that about this place," I say, not missing the way people in New York were all for themselves.

"You sure you're gonna be okay if I leave? I can call someone to come sit with you?" he says, looking me up and down once again like he's worried I'm going to just fall over.

"I will be fine. I'll go get cleaned up and nap for a bit and be good as new."

He looks unconvinced but walks over to the counter where Claire's notebook is sitting. "I better get this over to her before she thinks I forgot."

He walks out the door, throwing on his boots before leaning down, grabbing the trash bag in his other hand.

"Layton?" I call out after him. "Thank you."

"I'll see you tomorrow. Hopefully feeling better," he says, smiling at me. "Go get some rest."

The door shuts softly, and silence takes over the house as I collapse on the table. Letting the tears stream down into a puddle beneath me. The internal cracks grow a little more as I desperately try to hold it all together.

Chapter Three

LAYTON

Most people hate their jobs. But I'm not most people..

One of my favorite places in the world is on this ranch. When Tyler asked if I wanted to help him manage this place, I couldn't have been happier. The work is hard, and I bitch just to keep things interesting, but honestly, I couldn't see myself anywhere else.

I walk up to one of the new calves laying alone in the field—Mom's nowhere to be found. It doesn't take me long to spot her standing to the side, looking at the calf like it is a monster.

"Really, Betty?" I say, rolling my eyes at her before walking over to the poor calf. We only have a couple named cows here. Betty is one of them, because she is probably our meanest heifer. She also has a spot on her side that's shaped like the letter *B* which is helpful to know to avoid her.

I eye her, waiting to see if she has any reaction at all to me approaching the calf, but she couldn't care less.

I scoop the calf into my arms, and it doesn't fight me—which isn't a good sign. I hurry it back to the Gator.

"No more babies for you, Betty, you're a shitty mom," I yell as I drive away.

I race through the field back to the barn, where my best friend, Tyler, is unloading hay from the back of his truck. Tyler owns this place with his younger brother, Luke. Magnolia Falls Ranch was his dad's before he passed. Tyler handles all the physical work, and Luke is the brains of it all. Thank God, because Tyler can barely work his phone, let alone figure out the taxes and shit. He hears me coming and whips around, throwing his arms in the air.

"Layton, slow the hell down!" he yells. *Clearly, something is up his ass again today.* "I tell you all the time, this isn't a racetrack and you still drive around here like there's a fire."

"Will you stop bitching and help me?" I say. "Or better yet, go hang out with Betty. You can be assholes together."

I hop out of the seat, walking to the back and lift the calf out.

"I'm guessing he was born sometime last night. I gotta get back out and make sure we have no other unfit mamas. I got most of the field done. Can you make sure he gets something to eat?" I ask Tyler, who is now rubbing the back of his neck.

I don't wait for his response. I just shove the calf in his arms and hop back into the Gator, ready to take off.

"Layton," Tyler yells out. "Sorry, man, I just had a rough night. I'm an asshole."

"It's all good. I get it. This place is a lot of work. Maybe you need to get some ass. It will loosen you up. I know this hot little blonde with big blue eyes. I give her a ride to work every day because my buddy's an idiot." I laugh before speeding off.

"I take it back. You're an asshole," he shouts after me.

I laugh even harder knowing I just pissed him off more than he already was. It's not my fault he met a beautiful girl and instead of trying to make anything out of it, he's acting like a child. I know he feels like he shouldn't be happy since his younger brother's accident. An accident he swears he caused, even though he almost died that night. The whole situation was a nightmare. Luke never walked again, and the Tyler I knew died that night. He's done nothing but work since then.

I know why he feels the way he does, but I've also sat so many nights listening to Luke beg him to chill out. I'm not sure he even knows how to do that at this point.

I slowly pull into the field and drive over every inch, looking for any other things that need to be addressed before I head out for the day. Once I'm sure everything is good, I drive back up to the barn.

"Hey, I'm heading out early. Eric, Matt, Theo—tomorrow you're working with me. I need help building the new pen for a couple more horses Tyler has coming from Texas. We have the week to get it done."

"Alright, boss," Eric says, wiping the sweat off his face, leaving a line of mud in its path before pointing to the stall next to me. "What's the deal with the calf?"

I peek over the closed gate to see the small black and white pile of fluff curled in a ball surrounded by fresh straw. At least he's sleeping peacefully now.

"Found him this morning. Betty left the poor dude all alone. He seems like he's okay, but you know how it is. Hopefully, he makes it through the night," I say, taking another look at him before smacking my hands against the wooden gate. "Alright, guys, have a good night, drive safely, and don't do anything I wouldn't do."

"Damn, that leaves a lot of options, boss." Matt laughs as I walk away.

Thankfully, Tyler is leaning on his truck with his cell phone pressed against his ear when I walk up to mine. He locks eyes on me, holding a finger up.

"Just figure it out. You told me last week you'd have guys up here to help." He pauses, listening to the other person and I can see his jaw tensing with each word being said and how I wish I could hear the words. "I can't wait another week. I already lost three heifers. I don't know what you're not understanding about that. I needed them here last week. I paid for them to be here last week." He's silent again as he listens. "You know what, don't even bother sending them down. You're wasting my time," he says, hanging up the phone.

"Damn, what's that about?"

"This is why I don't hire outside help. No one gives a shit like we do. I tried to get some extra hands to get the heifers to the new pasture before this heat wave. He's got a million excuses for why they keep pushing it off."

"Screw 'em. We'll figure it out. Might have to pull some extra hours, but we will get them down there," I reassure him.

"I hate losing animals, man. Especially for things that could have been avoided."

"You can't change the weather. Who would have thought we'd have a heat wave this late in the year?"

"I know," he says before shoving off of his truck bed. "Did you need something?"

"Nah, I'm just heading out early. Everything's done, but I forgot I needed to pick something up on the way home."

"No problem. How's your mom? Is the treatment still going okay?" he asks, suddenly sounding worried. I know to expect these questions, but they still suck to answer.

How do I say yes? The treatments seem to work, but they are also making my mom a shell of the woman she was. I spend every night holding her hair while she pukes, and she can barely keep her eyes open most of the time.

"Yeah, seems to be helping."

"Good, glad to hear it. Tell mama I said hi."

It doesn't take me long to finish up before I'm hopping in my truck and heading into town. I drive down the endless empty roads until I come up to the small bakery. The white sign over the top of the worn building with the two cupcakes on the side reads *Mrs. B's Sweet Treats*. There is not a soul here this time of day with everyone working, but I know in a couple hours the line will be out the door.

The soft ding of the bell above the door breaks through the music playing inside.

"Layton, is that you, boy?" Mrs. B's voice carries from behind the counter. "Oh honey, you haven't stopped by in so long. You are becoming skin and bones," she says as she makes her way around the counter.

I look down to make sure we are both seeing the same man as she wraps her arms around me.

"Mrs. B, I've never been skin and bones; we both know that."

Mrs. B babysat me as a kid and is the reason for my country-boy-strong physique. She was constantly baking, and I was the best taste tester around. Still, twenty-five years later, she spoils me with way too many sweets.

"You stop that and come pick something out," she tells me as she walks back behind the counter.

"I actually have a special request. I need a bagel with cream cheese. I figured I could go to the store, but I thought I'd ask you first, since I'm sure fresh baked would be better."

"When do you need it?" she asks me.

"As soon as I can?"

"Well, come on boy, come wash them dirty hands and learn something."

I laugh but walk behind the counter, scrubbing my hands under the sink.

"How's your mama? I've been praying for her," she says as she puts a giant bowl on the counter in front of me.

"She's been doing better. Treatments have been tiring her out, but doctors seem optimistic with results so far," I tell her, trying to hide the slight choke in my voice.

There is something about watching a person you love battle cancer that withers away a piece of you. Cancer doesn't give a shit how many people love you, or if you are the sweetest damn person in the entire world. It will dig its claws so deeply into anyone it chooses and shred them apart while they fight with everything they are to destroy it.

"Baby, your mama is a fighter." Miss B's voice breaks through my fog and I realize she's already dumped a bunch of ingredients in the bowl in front of me.

"I know. It still doesn't make it fair that she has to go through it at all. She's been fighting her entire life. She raised me alone—put up with all my shit. She should be out there living, enjoying this part of her life. It's not fair."

Miss. B smiles sadly at me as she tosses some flour down on the counter in front of us before grabbing the ball of dough from the bowl.

"I can do the kneading, Miss B," I say to her, softly scooting her to the side so I can work the dough.

"Layton, if you ever need to talk, you're always welcome here. I watched my Robby fight. He sacrificed so much for us during Vietnam. When he finally came home, I thought the days of fighting were done. Fifteen years later, he was diagnosed with lung cancer. There were many nights the chemo had him so sick he couldn't get up by himself. There were so many days I thought I was going to lose him. I would spend the days giving every piece of myself to take care of him and our kids, and then spend the night crying myself to sleep. It changed me, and it will change you, too. Make sure you are talking to people. If I could go back, the only thing I would change is how I shut myself away from the world. I needed people more than ever, but I made myself feel like I had to do it on my own. You, dear, don't have to do this on your own and you don't always have to be so strong."

"Thank you," I say. "I don't have it in me today, Miss. B. But I am glad Mr. Rob's still here. I can't imagine who I'd be without him dragging me around the farm growing up."

"Drag you he did," she chuckles. "I remember the first time you went out drinking and called him to pick you up, then he woke you up at five to feed the horses. I thought you were going to puke all day long."

"He never got mad at me that night. Just said, 'You gotta be tough if you're gonna be stupid boy. See you at five.'" I laugh at the memory.

"He's always had a way with words."

"Well, let's let this dough rise, then we can shape it and bake it. In the meantime, I have three dozen first birthday cupcakes to ice in baby pink frosting. I'd love your help."

Three hours later, I am looking at a perfect bagel.

"Let that cool on the ride. Here is some cream cheese. Keep it separate so it doesn't melt," Mrs. B says. "Now, come here and give me a hug before you leave and I don't see you for another few months."

"I'll come back; I promise," I tell her, wrapping her in a hug. "Thank you for everything today. I needed it."

"You're welcome. Don't forget what I said about talking."

Chapter Four

TRISH

A soft knock breaks me from my fog as I open my eyes. After Layton left this morning, I got a quick shower and curled up on the couch with a book. The book that is still opened on page one across my chest. I stand, causing Charlie—Claire's bald cat—to run across the room and fly under the couch like he saw a monster. I'm sure I won't see him again for at least another month. At first, I wasn't his biggest fan. The first couple of weeks, he freaked me out. Now, I wake up every other day to a dead mouse by my door. Gross but helpful, so he's growing on me.

"Coming," I yell as I walk to the front door, unlocking the deadbolt and swinging it open to a face I didn't expect to see.

Layton stands on the other side with a white paper bag in his hand and a huge smile across his face.

"Good, you got some sleep. You look like you're feeling better." He says, holding the bag up to me. "I got you a bagel."

I don't move. I don't invite him in. I just stare at the white bag before letting my eyes drift past it to the man taking up the entire doorway. He's changed into a plain blue t-shirt and jeans with a belt and cowboy boots. I have to look up to see his face, where I see a well-groomed beard and cowboy hat. This morning, I didn't have time to fully appreciate him. He's nothing like Brett. He's not clean cut. He doesn't look like he spends hours at the gym or takes those stupid selfies in the mirror with the cut-out tank tops. He's strong—but in a rugged way. A way that makes me imagine how easily he could pick me up and do whatever he wanted with me.

What is my problem? I make a mental note to charge Buzz tonight since it's becoming obvious the lack of orgasms are getting to my head.

"Darlin', you're going to have to stop staring at me like that—turnin' all red and shit. Gonna, make me think your mind is in a dirty place. Don't get me wrong, I really like the idea of you thinking dirty things about me," he says with a teasing smirk, breaking all the thoughts in my mind.

"I—I was just..." I stutter out because I've never had a man be so blunt and all the thoughts in my mind just got so much dirtier. "Come in."

He laughs, following me inside. "I should have asked, but earlier you were saying how much you wanted one of these. I know a great bakery, so I swung in on my way home."

The smell from the bag hits me and my stomach grumbles.

"Please don't be sorry. I'm sorry for being so rude," I say, taking the bag from his hands.

"I hope it's okay. I know New York is famous for these things. They aren't as popular out here."

"It smells incredible," I say, unable to stop myself from ripping the bag open. I don't even bother with spreading the cream cheese on with a knife. I just rip a still warm piece off and drag it into it like a dip. Taking a bite, the most embarrassingly loud moan escapes me.

"Well, damn." Layton's voice breaks through my moment of pure bliss and I look up to his eyes locked on my mouth. "Um, like I said... I just, uh, wanted to get you that because you seemed like you might have wanted it or whatever." He blabbers out, his eyes still locked on my mouth.

"I'm so sorry. I don't know what's wrong with me," I gush. "This is seriously the best bagel I've ever had."

A smile lights his entire face up, replacing the hungry one that was just there.

"It's not the normal sick-food I think of. But hey, if it works, I'm glad to help. I have to go pick Claire up, but I just wanted to drop that off before I went to grab her," he says casually as he pushes away from the counter like he didn't just make my entire week better. He shoots me another smile, a dimple showing on one side of his face as he walks out the front door. "I'll see you tomorrow."

I'm left wondering what the hell just happened before running up the steps praying there is at least a little charge left in my friend.

I log onto my computer, going through the rest of my work for the day. Thankfully, everything seems quiet. The system I set up earlier seems to be holding strong—for now. I convinced myself when Claire got home I was going to talk to her, but I fell asleep. By the time I woke up, her door was shut, and I was sure she was out.

My phone rings on the bed next to me.

"Hey, Mom," I say, answering without even looking at the screen. She's the only one that would call me at five in the morning since she seems oblivious to the time change between us.

"You got more mail today. I told you to contact the post office years ago about this, Trish. It's not as easy as to get these to you as it was when you were close," she complains.

"Hey, Mom, I miss you too," I say sarcastically.

"Trish, this isn't a joke. It's annoying to have to get your mail every single day."

"I'm trying to get it fixed. You should have thought about that before you named me after you."

"Well, if I had known you'd be nothing like me, I would have," she snips back.

I try to ignore the burn that comes with the insult, but it's hard.

"I'll try again," I tell her.

"Good. I saw Brett yesterday," she says, and I instantly freeze.

"You didn't tell him anything, did you?"

"No," I can see her rolling her eyes through the phone. "I just don't understand. He's devastated, honey. He said you didn't even tell him you were leaving. He woke up to you gone. That poor boy was good to you, and he is a shoo-in to take over his dad's business."

"You wouldn't understand, Mom."

"You're right, I don't. I swear you are bound and determined to destroy your life."

"He hurt me."

"That?" she says, appalled. "That silly misunderstanding is why you left?"

"Yeah, Mom, him almost killing me would be the reason."

"For the love of God, Trish, you are so dramatic. You know he didn't mean to do that," she says. "Do you know how much money you walked away from? People would've looked at you on his arm and been so jealous. You were so close to my dream life."

"You date him then. I never wanted that life," I say, only half paying attention as I dig through my closet for a hoodie.

"I give up. You never take anything seriously. I really hope you're happy out there, because this life won't be waiting when you come back," she snaps before hanging up.

I throw the phone on my bed, pulling the hoodie over my head and flopping down next to it. "I guess it's a good thing I'm never going back."

I stare across the room at the unopened box of red hair dye sitting on the counter across from me. It's as close to my natural color as I could find. I've held off opening it because part of me is terrified I'll see the girl that was never enough. My mom hated my red hair growing up, but I didn't dye it until after I started seeing Brett. I've absolutely hated it ever since.

Every time I look in the mirror, I see the woman they built. The expensive clothes, fake blonde hair, the lie I had to become to make them happy. I'm fed up with it all. I climb from the bed, grabbing the box, and head into the bathroom.

As I stare at myself in the mirror, I realize I don't even know who I am anymore.

"This is freedom," I tell myself as I mix the dye and begin chaotically squirting it on my head. I can't help but smile as the bright white disappears beneath the red goop. I rub it in until every single spot of white is gone. I sit on the closed lid of the toilet, pulling up my mom's contact info and hit block. I'm sure I'll unblock her at some point, but right now, I want to erase it all. I can't deal with all of the lies that have dragged me under for years. While everyone else smiled at the woman I'd become, I was drowning to live up to the expectations that surrounded her.

Chapter Five

LAYTON

"Mom?" I shout through the quiet house. I'm greeted with the soft sniffles from the other room.

I rush towards the sound, finding her sitting on the floor of the living room surrounded by photo albums with tears streaming down her cheeks.

"What's wrong?" I ask her, taking in the scene.

She jumps at the sound of my voice, looking up to lock eyes on me. Her hand flying to her chest. "Layton, I didn't hear you come in."

"I brought you dinner."

She looks to the window as if in shock that the sky is ink black.

"I hadn't realized it was so late," she says, not bothering to pull herself from the floor, her eyes going back to the photo in her hand. It's of her holding me when I was a baby. She had me dressed in some ridiculous fuzzy bear costume as she stared at me with a huge smile on her face. It was one of the few pictures of her from before dad met Kim and decided we weren't worth his time. You'd never know the hell she's gone through by the photo timeline she has spread across the floor. In every picture she stares at me like I hung the moon.

Last year, I finally convinced her to make an online dating profile. She found a lump the next day. Three weeks later, I sat holding her hand as the doctor ripped my world from beneath me.

Her once full frame is now much frailer. Her face, once bright with life, now seems broken and set with wrinkles that didn't exist last year. She has her favorite bandana wrapped around her head. It's white with vines and small yellow flowers covering it. I found it in a little farm store outside of town a couple of months back.

I walk over, sit next to her, and pull her into my side. She's under half my size now and basically disappears under my hold. I feel her sobs take over as she cries into my chest.

"What's going on, mama?" I ask her as she leans back to look at me. Her swollen red eyes looking me over.

"Baby, I want you to promise me something," she says, grabbing my face in her hands. "No matter what happens to me, you live. Okay? You have spent the last year sacrificing everything to take care of me. I want you to go out and enjoy life. These years fly by, and you can never get them back. You are an amazing man. I don't want you to miss out on life because of me."

"Mom, you're going to be okay," I say, a slight edge to my voice that I don't mean to come out.

"I had an appointment today. I got the call a few days ago that I needed to come in. The treatments stopped working, and the cancer has spread. I have a couple of options, but the truth is the doctors aren't optimistic."

"They said the treatments *were* working," I argue.

"I know, baby," she whispers.

"Why didn't you tell me? I would have been there," I say, pulling her back into me, afraid to let go. Afraid of what this means. "I could have been there."

"I didn't want to upset you and I heard you saying this week was crazy with the cows and moving them. I know you guys lost a few in this heat. I didn't want to add more to your plate," she says, relaxing into my side. "Plus, I am your mama. I am a big girl. I love having your support, but sometimes I need to take care of myself."

"You know that's bullshit. I will always take care of you," I say, my voice low as her breathing evens out.

My mind screams with questions about what this means. Instead of begging for answers, I sit staring at the pictures in front of me. The past seeming like a weapon teasing to the fact that this may be all I have soon. Dinner is sitting on the counter, but I'm no longer hungry. I let it go bad as I stare at the past all night long, the only thread I have left tucked into my side.

"What the hell were you thinking?" I yell at Derek as he gets up from the ground, brushing his pants off.

We've been at this all day, and the kid can't get it. Normally I'm the most patient, that's why Tyler asked me to come out and work with him today. Apparently, I'm the fifth guy he's trained with this week and from the looks of it, he hasn't learned shit. Now he just kicked the shit out of poor Pearl, and he's lucky she didn't kill his dumbass with the way she reared back and threw him off of her.

I knew I should have told Tyler I don't have it in me today. I would much rather be beating the shit out of my body. Drowning out the thoughts and millions of questions left unanswered as I carried my mom to her bed last night and downed the rest of the bottle of Jack.

Every ounce of patience has flown out the window. I can handle a lot of shit, but hurting our animals isn't one of them. It's taking everything in me not to slap Derek across the back of his head.

"Theo said that's the only way to get 'em to listen."

"Theo's an asshole," I say, annoyed. "Have you ever seen Theo ride a horse?"

"No."

"Exactly, because the idiot can't stay on."

"I can't do this. I've been out here for days trying to ride in a circle, for God's sake."

Guilt kicks in for snapping at him. I know he's only twenty and wasn't raised around this shit. His parents are some rich bastards that are never home. Derek's a good kid but he grew up spoiled rotten. I'll give him credit, he refuses to live on their money. He comes here every day and works harder than anyone else trying to save up to have his own life. I like the kid, but he scares the shit out of me some days.

"You're going to get it, but not like that. Come here," I say, walking over to grab the reins. "The problem is you're being too aggressive. You're stressing her out. You gotta chill."

I reach up, petting her soft fur and calming her down.

"No more riding today. Your new job is to get her to respect you. You treat them right, and they will treat you right. Grab her reins," I tell him, and he quickly reaches out to snatch them from me.

I move my hand away, taking the reins with me.

"What did I just say? Calmly," I say, handing them back to him.

"Sorry," he says, taking the reins from my hand.

"Now, walk her around the pasture a couple times. She has to learn she can trust you," I say, watching the skittish kid as he starts walking, and chuckling to myself when the horse stands firm. I walk up next to him, gesturing for her to follow. She immediately perks up and starts trotting. "Walk her a couple laps then put her up. Tomorrow, we start fresh. From here on out, no one else teaches you. You hear me? Not if that shit you pulled earlier is what they're showin' you. If I see you do anything like that again, you won't ride another horse at this ranch."

"Yes, sir," he says. I hate how he calls me sir. It makes me feel old as hell, but I don't correct him. "Where are you going?"

"Me and Theo are going to have a little talk," I say, walking away.

I make it to Theo in half the time I should, and by the time I get to him, I'm beyond pissed. Pissed at him for being a piece of shit. Pissed that he could have killed Derek. Pissed in general. Pissed enough that I'm about to let my temper get the best of me.

"Hey, boss. I was just telling the guys about the two girls I brought home last night—" His voice is all I need to boil over the edge.

I wrench back and crash my fist right into his nose. The sound of the bone breaking fills my ears. It doesn't make me feel any better.

"What the fuck?" he yells, instantly raising his fist to fight back. I get right in his face, daring him too. I beg him to give me a reason to let out the rage simmering inside of me. He backs down, reaching up to grab his face as blood pours down his hands looking at me in shock.

"Pack your shit."

"What?" he squeals. "Layton, I need this job."

"Should have thought about that."

"I'll call Tyler," he argues.

I laugh, "Please do, I'll wait. You can tell him how you told Derek to *kick the fuckin'* horse to get her respect. I would love to hear Tyler's response to that shit."

"You don't know what you're talking about."

"I don't? So, did you not tell Derek to kick the horse?"

"I—" he says, pausing.

"That's what I thought. Here's the thing, Theo. I haven't liked you since the first day you stepped foot on this ranch. You're a lazy piece of shit. You risking one of my men's safety is inexcusable."

He looks around at the rest of the guys to have his back, but they all look down at their boots. They all hate him, too. I've overheard them time and time again. He comes from money like Derek, but it turned him into an entitled prick. He walks around this ranch like he's king. No one likes that out here. I know I took it too far by hitting him. I'm sure I'll catch hell for it later, but I can't seem to care right now.

"Let's go. I'll make sure you find your way out," I say. "You guys get back to work."

Watching Theo walk off of the property actually makes me feel a little better.

Chapter Six

TRISH

I pull an old T-shirt I've had for years over my head, a band's logo on the front. Part of me is sad as I do. The suitcase I left behind was the one that had all of my makeup, nice clothes, and hair stuff. I would have cried if it had been the one I stuffed all my t-shirts in, though. Brett hated them. He insisted I wear girl clothes. Come to think about it, before him I didn't give a shit about how I looked. I had long outgrown the days of thick eyeliner and pin straight hair from high school, and I was completely content with the messy bun and comfy clothes that enraged my mother.

It didn't take him long to comment on how I looked. Simple comments I never over thought.

"You know your eyes would look so much nicer if you wore makeup to make them stand out."

"You have such a nice body; you shouldn't hide it under those ugly shirts you always wear."

At first, I ignored the comments. It was nothing my mom hadn't said before. They got meaner the longer we stayed together, to the point he would refuse to leave the house with me if I wasn't done up. It didn't matter if we were just running out to the grocery store. When he got home from work, he expected me to look 'put together', or he'd sleep in the spare room. So I changed. I loved him, and I wanted everyone to leave me alone.

Why was I such an idiot? It feels like the longer I'm away, the more the fog lifts. And now that I can see clearly, I'm realizing just how bad it really was.

I look myself over in the mirror—a clean face, sprinkled with soft freckles and my red hair tossed into a bun on top of my head. I can't help but smile at the woman staring back at me. It's been so long since I've seen her. I know getting her to stay will take time, but I am desperate to keep her. To wake up every day and live without wondering if every choice I make is good enough for the people around me. I quickly throw on a pair of black leggings and shove on my flip-flops before running down the steps grabbing my purse.

As soon as I step out the front door, Layton pulls into the driveway.

"Hey," he says, jumping from the truck. "How are you feeling today?"

"So much better. I think that bagel really helped. It's the first thing I've held down all week," I tell him as I throw my phone in my bag.

"Your hair," he says.

I look up to catch his eyes scanning down my body, then back up to my face. I instantly regret every choice I made. All of my insecurities rush forward as I feel my face heating up.

"I know, I'm sorry. I dyed it back to my natural color. I can go change and throw on some makeup. I don't have much. I left most of it behind. I have some stuff, though," I stammer, instantly reverting back to the person I just promised myself I wouldn't. "I just thought since we were only going to the store, I could wear something comfortable."

"Woah, you're fine," he says, locking on my face, his eyebrows drawn in confusion. "Why the hell would you think you needed to do that?"

I shoot my eyes to the ground, anxiety setting in. I want to run back into the house.

"Trish," he says gently, putting his finger under my chin and lifting my face to his. "I have no clue what the hell just went through that head of yours, but I was checking you out. You look hot." I feel myself unconsciously lean into the touch as he brushes a fallen lock of hair behind my ear.

"I know I shouldn't go out without getting done up."

"I don't know who told you that dumb shit. You be you. Don't let anyone make you feel less for that, yeah?"

I stare into his eyes as they seem to hold mine. "Yeah."

"Good girl. Now let's go fill that fridge," he says, letting my chin go leaving my jaw to drop to the ground.

I pinch myself, causing a slight pain to erupt in my arm. *Yup, this is definitely real life.*

I look up to Layton, who is standing at the passenger door, his one eyebrow cocked up in question. "Did you just pinch yourself?" he asks.

"I thought maybe I got sucked into my book when I fell asleep yesterday," I say as I walk over, climbing into the truck.

"I have no idea what that means," he says, looking confused before he just shuts the door and walks around the front of the truck.

"What have you eaten today?" he asks as he pulls the truck out onto the road.

"I just had a bowl of peas."

He shakes his head at me. "Good thing we are going shoppin' then."

"Does your boss know you've left early two days in a row?" I ask, worried I might be getting him in trouble.

"My boss is my best friend and he owes me right now, since he refuses to pick Claire up."

"Why is that?" I ask. "She was so sure he liked her."

"He does like her. That's the problem."

"I don't understand."

"Tyler has a lot of shit on his plate he doesn't like to talk about. He's been punishing himself for years, and I don't know if he knows how to stop. I hope he figures it the hell out though, because he is an idiot for not going after Claire. That was the happiest I've ever seen him."

"Claire too," I say sadly as Layton pulls into the parking lot.

"That's enough of that depressing shit. Let's go," he says, opening his door, "Girl, just gimme a damn second," he says as I reach for my door before he walks over to my side to open mine. I am so not used to the people out here and how nice they are.

"I'll meet you back at the truck when you're done. No rush."

I look at the cart full of random stuff. I know they say you shouldn't shop hungry, but I didn't have much of a choice today. The cashier hands me my change, and I push the cart out to the parking lot. Layton leans against the back of his truck and looks my way. As soon as he sees me, a smile lights up his face.

"I'm sorry I took so long. I should have made a list."

"You're fine. I told you not to rush," he says, grabbing a bag, looking inside and setting it in the bed of his truck. "Go hop in the truck, I have the air on for you, so it should be cool."

"I can help."

"I know you can, but you don't have too," he says as I watch him look in another bag. I want to ask him why he's inspecting everything I bought, but he opens a cooler and puts the bag in it. "There is a sandwich on your seat. It's egg salad. I hope that's okay. I had no idea what you liked, so I went with my mom's favorite. If you want something different, I'll run back in."

That's enough to get me moving. My stomach growls loudly at the mention of food.

"I'll take that as a yes?"

"It sounds so good!" I say. "But I still feel like I should help."

"Trish, go eat. I finished mine already."

"Okay," I say, walking over and jumping into the passenger seat then ripping open the white wrapping and taking a bite. Layton's mom has great taste. This sandwich is incredible.

It only takes a couple of minutes before Layton hops in the driver-seat with his phone pressed to his ear.

"I'm on my way right now. Thank you for letting me know," he says before shoving his phone in his pocket. His entire demeanor has shifted. "I gotta swing in and check on my mom really quick."

"No problem. Is everything okay?" I ask, though I'm not sure why when it's clear something is wrong.

"I'm not sure. Her neighbor goes to check on her every day and she didn't answer the door. I'm just worried," he says, speeding out onto the road.

He flies down the street, and I thank God we are in the middle of nowhere and there are no other cars on the road to hold us up. The more we drive, the more the silence eats at my thoughts. I'm not sure what is going on with his mom, but it's clear he's worried about her. His knuckles are white as he grips the steering wheel and uses the other hand to hit her name on his phone for the third time. Once again, it goes to voicemail.

He turns into a driveway leading up to a small white house before throwing the truck into park and jumping out. I follow behind, unsure what else to do. He rushes inside the house yelling, "Mom!" over and over and a piece of my heart breaks with the fear in his voice.

I go to follow him inside when something catches my eye on the side of the house. I look over to see a small woman leaning over in a flower bed with her back towards me.

"Layton!" I yell. "I think I found her." I run up to the woman, placing my hand on her shoulder gently causing her to jump.

She looks at me, face marred in confusion as she takes me in. I realize how crazy I must look, coming up to her like this. I hear Layton run up behind me as the woman reaches up, yanking a small headphone from her ear.

"Holy shit, mom!" Layton says, collapsing in front of her wrapping her in his arms.

I see the dark circles under her eyes. The bandana tied around her head. The fear pouring off of Layton and I realize he thought he lost her. I take a step back, letting them have their space.

"Layton, what's the matter with you?" she asks him.

"Evelynn said she came over and couldn't find you. You weren't answering your phone. I thought something happened," he says, still trying to calm himself down.

"I've been out here all day. I wanted to get some fresh air. I was getting cooped up inside."

"You gotta keep your phone on you, okay?" he tells her.

"I'm sorry I scared you. I promise, from now on, I will keep my phone on me." She looks over at me again and her entire face lights up before she stands wiping her dirt covered hands on her pants. "Who's this?"

Layton stands up, reaching out to help pull her up with him.

"This is Trish. She just moved out here from New York a few months ago with Claire."

"It's so nice to meet you, Trish." She smiles. "Since you guys are here, would you like some dessert? I just took out some cobbler."

"Mom, you are doing a lot today," Layton says, helping walk her to the door.

"Once they start these new treatments, I'm going to be sick again like last time. I just want to have a week of living before then," she tells him, smiling softly.

I see his heartache as he looks at her. "Okay, mama, cobbler sounds amazing. Trish, do you have time?"

"I have nothing but time." I say, smiling.

Chapter Seven

LAYTON

"He carried that thing around in his pocket until he was fourteen." My mom laughs, pointing to the small scrap of blanket clenched tightly in my hand in one of the pictures.

"Awe, that's so sweet," Trish gushes as they both look over to me and I thank God I brought the cooler for the food because this is the most I've seen my mom laugh in years.

"He's always been my sweet boy. I don't know where I'd be without him," she says softly.

"You definitely have raised a great man from what I've seen the last day I've known him," Trish says as she laughs.

My mom yawns and lays her head back against the couch. I know she's exhausted. She overdid it today, but I also can't argue with her. Last time she went through chemo, it made it so she could barely function. Trish notices the shift, too and looks over at me, wordlessly expressing that we should wrap up.

"Ms. Kilier, thank you so much for inviting me in for dessert. It was amazing and I can honestly say I haven't had such a fun night in a long time," she says, rising from the couch.

"Oh, honey, I loved having you. I really hope you come back again soon," my mom says, fighting her eyes open.

Trish only replies with a smile as my mom drifts off to sleep.

We both quickly clean up before I carry her to her bed. The walk to the truck is quiet. Trish hasn't stopped staring at her feet since I walked out.

"Hey, you okay?" I ask her.

"You are so lucky to have such an amazing mom. She seriously may be the nicest person I ever met."

"She really is the best. I hate leaving her alone all day. The ranch is just so busy this time of year. I know Tyler would give me more time off, but he needs the help."

"I could do it," she says. "Well, I'd have to figure out how to get over here, but I wouldn't mind hanging out with her."

"I can't ask you to do that."

"I wouldn't mind at all. It gets lonely being home by myself."

"I could pick you up in the mornings and bring you here, then drop you back off on the way home. It would line up perfectly actually, since my mom is closest to the ranch."

"Shit! Claire!" she says suddenly. "She didn't have a ride. You were supposed to give her a ride."

"It's okay, I texted Tyler when I found out I had to come here. He got her," I say. "I'm hoping he pulled his head out of his ass."

"Are you sure you won't have to go out of your way to bring me here? I want to help, not be more of a pain."

"Are you kidding me? You would help me so much. You have no idea how distracted I am worrying about her. If you were here, I'd feel so much better," I reassure her.

"Okay, then yes, I seriously would love to come here during the week," she says happily.

"I'll talk to her about it tomorrow, and then we can figure out the rest."

I open the door, watching her climb in, trying to ignore the fact that I want to shove her against the side of my truck and kiss the shit out of her.

The drive home is quiet as Trish stares out the window, lost in thought. I do the same thing my mind lost in the thoughts of way too many what-ifs.

The fear from earlier crashes back into me. For a moment I thought I'd lost her. I have never felt fear like that.

Before I know it, I'm pulling into Trish's driveway. The house is completely dark, and I wonder how Tyler made out with Claire.

I jump out, running around the front of the truck and open the passenger door for Trish.

"I'll get the door," she says, digging through her bag before walking over to unlock the house.

"How 'bout you start unpacking, and I'll bring in the rest," I say as I drop the first load on the counter.

She smiles, grabbing the bags from the counter and starts unloading them into the fridge. It doesn't take long before we've silently unpacked everything.

"I guess Tyler and Claire kissed and made up,"

"I hope so. He's been a miserable ass," I chuckle as I reach for the cabinet I saw her put a box in there earlier. I should just hand it to her. Instead, I come up behind her just far enough away I'm not touching any piece of her and open the cabinet above her head. I hear her suck in a sharp breath and she freezes, hands still wrapped tightly around the edge of the counter. I should know better, since visions of her played over in my head all last night. I'd be an idiot not to acknowledge how hot she is. I want to touch her. Flip her around and pull those tight ass leggins off, put that pretty little ass on the counter and have my way with her. If she were any other woman, I would have already seen how far she would let me go. I'm no gentleman and I see how she looks at me—how her cheeks blush, how she clenches her thighs together.

This can't be like that, though. My mom loves her, and she just offered her time to make sure she's safe. That's like a bucket of ice water over me. I quickly step back, running my hand through my hair.

"Layton," Trish says softly, and I slam my eyes shut.

"Yeah, darlin'?"

"Thank you for today." She twists around so she's facing me.

"Anytime," I say, her heated cheeks and neck making it so much harder to walk away. "I should head home."

"Yeah, Claire will probably be home soon, I'm sure." I take another step back, distancing myself from her enough to break us both from our stare. "Put your number in and text yourself so you can let me know what your mom says about me coming over," she says handing me her phone. As I hand it back to her, I force myself to say goodnight and leave before I make a choice I can't take back.

"Okay good, now gently throw your leg over her back," I say to Derek who finally seems to be getting the hang of riding. Last night was the first full night of sleep I've had in weeks, and I'm grateful for it as the sun beats on my back and I think of the full day ahead of me. "Way better. See what happens when you treat 'em right?" I say, watching him finally trot around the loop on a horse.

"I still think I could have done this days ago," he argues.

"Maybe, but you also kicked my horse, so letting you go right back at it wouldn't have taught you a damn thing."

He whispers something under his breath that I don't catch when my phone rings. My mom's name lights the screen.

"The house is ready!" she says gleefully.

"Mom, I told you Trish wouldn't have cared about the house. She saw it last week." I was hoping to get Trish over to my mom's right away. Mom, of course, insisted on having someone come in and clean first. I'm sure it'll look exactly the same as it did before since it wasn't dirty.

"Oh, honey, I can't wait for her to come. I'm going to bake us some snacks. I know the end of next week is my first chemo. I may have her skip the next day. You know how I get afterwards," she rambles.

"Mom, she's not going to care, she's just coming to hang out with you. You don't gotta stress yourself out," I tell her, keeping an eye on Derek.

"I know, but I haven't had a friend in a long time. I know she's younger, but it is going to be nice to have someone around to talk to. I really like her," she says. "Maybe you should ask her on a date? It's been a while since you've been out."

"Mom, It's not like that."

"It could be."

"It can't. I got too much going on right now to date."

"I just don't want you to miss out because of me. You aren't getting any younger, and I'm not going to be here forever—"

"I love you, mom, but I gotta get back to work." I can't listen to it anymore.

"Okay, baby. I'm sorry. I'll see you later," she tells me before hanging up.

I feel guilty for not letting her talk, but I can't think about her not making it through this.

"Alright let's take her down to the falls." I tell Derek as I hop on my horse.

"Finally."

The sun beats down on the fields in front of us, making them almost seem as if they are glowing. The only sounds filling the air are the birds chirping and the soft mooing of the cows as they stand by their babies in the distant fields.

I hope this is what Heaven looks like. The thought of nothingness being all there is next, is unfathomable to me. I can't picture the most amazing woman I know stuck between this hell she's living and nothing. The only thing that keeps me from going crazy is imagining the glow, the healing, and the peace that comes with *him* really being up there.

No matter how hard I try to shove the thoughts of life after her away, they always come back. Now that the treatments have stopped working, my mind is never silent. It's as if a constant battle is raging inside me between the potentials of the future. You know as a child one day you will lose your parents, but you never expect it to be when they are young and still so full of life. When she went into chemo the first time, she still seemed healthy on the outside. She was youthful for her age. She had this long brown hair that I loved as a kid because it glowed under the sun. Chemo stole all of that. Just when she finally started to get some of it back, it decides to rear its ugly head. The only thing is this time I don't know how she will make it through the brutality of it all.

I swallow down the lump in my throat. I'm not alone, and I won't sit here and cry in front of Derek.

Kid has enough shit, he doesn't need a full-grown man breaking down in front of him.

    As the falls come into view, I think to myself, *this is definitely what Heaven looks like.*

Chapter Eight

TRISH

I scroll through my emails, making sure I didn't miss anything from yesterday before closing my laptop. I'm finally getting my feet back under me with work, and thankfully my clients have noticed it too. I broke down and sent an apology a few days ago telling them things got a little crazy, but it's all sorted out. They thanked me for my honesty and said they felt like something was off over the last couple months but they were glad to see the improvement and to hear that things were settling down. I was so thankful they didn't give up on me.

My phone lights up and Layton's name fills the screen and I answer it.

"Good morning, darlin'." his voice comes through the line and instantly brings a smile to my face.

"Good morning."

"My mom called, she's excited to have you come, her house is *finally clean*." He laughs.

"Her house wasn't even dirty."

"I tried to tell her that, but she's trying to make a good impression."

"Awe, well, I'm excited to go hang out with her."

"Have you had anything to eat yet today?" he asks me and I look down at the phone to realize it's almost lunch and I haven't even had breakfast yet.

"I have not."

"If you're not busy, I can come pick you up. I gotta run to Brookside to pick up some supplies for the ranch. There is a place out there that makes the best burgers and shakes. We can get lunch before we head back. It's about a twenty-minute drive if you want to come with me."

"A burger sounds amazing."

"Great, I'll be there in five minutes."

"I don't have time to get ready," I say.

"Are you dressed?"

"Yeah,"

"Well, we're going to be in the truck most of the trip, and I don't think the burger joint has a dress code. Just get your cute ass outside."

"I don't think I've ever met a man like you," I say smiling as I walk to the mirror and run a brush through my hair while taking a second to look at my huge t-shirt and biker shorts.

"What do you mean?"

"I've just never met someone so blunt," I say walking out the door to see he's already in the yard walking to the passenger door. He's a mess, but it works for him. I know it's wrong, but I let my eyes travel all the way down his body until I close the distance between us and have to look up to his face. It's only then that I finally pull the phone away from my ear. I see him smirk. He knows I just checked him out.

"You don't like that I'm honest with you?" he asks, and I feel the warmth in my face.

"It's not that. I just... I don't think anyone's ever talked to me like you do."

"No one ever told you that you were cute?"

I look to the ground because when he says it like that, it seems completely absurd. He moves in so his boots are almost touching my sandals.

"I mean, I guess."

He cocks an eyebrow. "You shouldn't have to guess. You're cute, beautiful, sexy—all of it. Fuck whoever made you question that."

"You don't know me," I argue as I break eye contact, walking back around the front of the truck and climbing into the passenger seat.

"I don't have to know you to see that you're attractive as hell. Now let's go get you some food. You've gotta be starvin'," he says, closing the door and walking to the driver's side.

"Thank you for picking me up. I did actually have food at my house this time, so I wouldn't have starved."

"Maybe I wanted an excuse to see you again," he says, pulling out of the driveway. "You know? Make sure I didn't get a serial killer to hangout with my mom."

"Your plan to decide if I'm a murderer is to take me out to eat?"

"You can tell a lot about a person by the burger they choose."

"Oh really? And what burger will you be choosing?" I ask him, chuckling.

"I'm not sure. I try to mix it up."

"Fair enough."

We pull up to the restaurant, and Layton jumps from the truck walking to my side to open the door and helps me out. It's a small place, but pretty crowded for the middle of a weekday.

"What's that?" I ask him as we sit in our booth where a picture of a man hangs above a plaque that reads *Stuffed Burger Champions* with only one name etched into it.

"They have this massive stuffed burger. It has all kinds of random stuff on it like mozzarella sticks, fries, and chicken tenders. If you finish that and a shake, you don't have to pay for the burger and you win free fries and milkshakes for a year, a t-shirt," he points to the shirt that looks a hell of a lot like it says *Got Stuffed at Benny's,* "and your name on the wall."

"That sounds amazing."

"Get it." He shrugs.

"I don't know, that's a lot of food. I should probably get something a little healthier," I say checking the menu for a chicken sandwich.

"Do you want something healthier?" he asks.

I pause. I honestly hadn't thought about what I wanted. Anytime Brett and I would go out to eat, he would order me a salad or chicken. Now that I'm sitting here thinking about it, I realize how messed up that was.

"Actually, I really don't."

"Then get the burger."

"What if I can't finish it?"

"Then we pack it up and you finish it later."

"You guys ready to order?" The waitress says as she walks up to our table.

"I'll take the Stuffed Benny with a chocolate shake." I see a couple heads whip around towards me, and the waitress raises her brows in question.

"Alright, and you?"

"I'll take the jalapeno popper burger, chocolate shake for me too."

She scribbles it down on the pad of paper in her hand and walks away.

"Do you think everyone's going to judge me when I don't finish this whole thing?" I ask him, feeling awkward.

"Maybe they will, but it doesn't matter. No matter what you do in life, people are going to judge you. You can either spend your entire life trying like hell to make them happy and fail, because it's impossible, or spend your life making *you* happy."

"What if I have no idea how to do that?" I ask him.

"Then you work at it. Every time you find yourself questioning if your choices are good enough for the people around you, ask why the hell the people around you need you to change yourself for their happiness."

I open my mouth to respond, but nothing comes out. My entire life I've been expected to be a certain way. The second I failed, I was blamed for their day being ruined. I can't remember the last time someone, aside from Claire, just let me be me. And before this moment I hadn't even realized that Claire was the only person that has ever actually seen the real me.

"Here are those burgers and shakes." The waitress's voice breaks through my thoughts as she sets a burger down in front of me. It's the size of my head, but it looks so good. It's been years since I've eaten anything this unhealthy, and my stomach growls in anticipation. I look up to Layton who is just smiling at me as he thanks the waitress.

"Eat as much as you want, and we will get a box for what's left—if there is anything." He says, taking a big bite of his burger.

I do the same and instantly regret all the stupid salads I've been forcing myself to eat. "This is amazing."

"I told you—best burgers around."

I'm going to blame the lack of grease in my diet over the last few years for the absolutely savage, uncaring way I eat. By the time I look up, Layton's plate is empty, and he is locked in on me with a look of shock on his face.

I look down at my plate to see every single speck of food gone. I was so caught up in talking and enjoying myself, I hadn't even realized I had somehow eaten it all.

You are disgusting, my mind screams. *You should do better. You have no self-control.* The spiral is coming. I feel it as Brett and my mom's voices fill my head. Their looks of disgust glaring at me.

"I think I might have just fallen in love with you." Layton's voice rings through.

I look up to see him smiling at me, not a hint of disgust on his face. Instantly the voices quiet, and I feel a little better being myself.

By the time I walk in the door, it's already dark outside. I have my new t-shirt on and have officially earned a picture on the wall at Benny's. The whole drive home we crack up at the number of men that ordered the burger as we were leaving determined that if a girl could do it—they could do it too.

Being with Layton is as easy as being with Claire. Something I took for granted all of these years, until Layton pointed it out. She's the only person in my life that's loved me for me and just wanted me to be happy. Instead of leaning on her, I let the people determined to hurt me shove her away.

Claire's sitting on the couch with a box opened in front of her and I realize she's finally going through some of Michael's stuff. The reality of how much I've missed her crashes into me. She looks up to me and I can't stop the tears that fall down my face.

I walk in, sitting down on the couch next to her. We spend the next hour looking through the box in front of us until we have it completely emptied.

"I miss him so much," she says in a voice just barely over a whisper.

"I know you do," I say, brushing my fingers through her hair. "Claire, I owe you an apology for how I've been acting. I honestly have no idea how to handle life anymore. I feel like for years I've just held it all together, but now, I just can't."

"I wish you never felt like you had to do that. I should have stepped in earlier. I should have seen it. The hair. The clothes. I was so worried I'd be like your mom, judging you for doing what you wanted—even though none of it made sense."

"It wasn't your fault; you were balancing so much of your own life. Honestly, even if you had said something, I was so blind I would have most likely not even seen the problem."

"He hurt you, Trish."

"He did," I confirm.

A sob escapes her. "I'm okay now. I'm safe."

"What happened?"

"He had a work party. He told me on the drive there that he didn't approve of how I looked," I tell her. "He hadn't even told me there was a party until an hour before it started. While we were there, he drank—a lot. More than I've ever seen him drink before. I kept to myself, worried I would make him angrier if I made myself stand out more than he felt I already had. He walked up and grabbed me by the arm an hour after we arrived. His dad saw him pulling me and stopped him, asking what the hell he was doing and told him he was causing a scene. I know he was just trying to help, but with every word out of his mouth, I could feel Brett's grip tightening against me." I suck in a breath, trying not to lose myself to the memory that night. "I honestly thought about telling his dad I was terrified to leave at that moment, but I kept my mouth shut. I'm not sure if that would have saved me or made it worse. Somehow, I convinced him to let me drive, but that didn't stop him from slapping me across the face. That was the first time he'd laid his hands on me. I made up my mind as soon as I got home that I was leaving. As soon as we walked inside, he grabbed a huge vase we had by the front door. I hated that thing from the minute he brought it into the house. Who needs a three-foot-tall vase that holds nothing? He threw it at me, just missing my head with the thing. I tried to run past him, but he tackled me to the ground, slamming my back against the floor. All I felt was burning through my back as my skin was torn to ribbons by the shards littering the floor. There was so much blood. I was sure I was going to die. I still have no clue how I woke back up. My mom was there, I had a bandage across my back and the floor was scrubbed clean."

"Your mom knew?" she says, full of hate.

"I guess Brett called her the next day when he woke up and saw I wasn't dead. I told her everything, but she believed his story over mine—big shocker. She refused to take me to the hospital and told me something like, 'This wouldn't look good for his future.'

For weeks, she fed me random painkillers and antibiotics she got from God knows where. By the time I healed, Brett was back to acting like the perfect man, and I was desperately trying to figure out how to leave."

"You should never have had to go through that by yourself," she says. "I would have been there for you."

"I know you would have, but you were already giving so much of yourself to save Michael. I was afraid any more stress would pull you under."

"I feel like I let you down."

"Are you serious? I feel like I let *you* down. I was so busy taking care of my life that I couldn't help you. I wanted to so badly. When you called and told me Michael died and I couldn't come to you, I was so angry with myself."

"You were trying to survive. Neither of us stopped loving the other. We were just trying our best to keep our heads above water."

"I don't know how I would have survived this life without you," I tell her.

"I couldn't have done it without you either," she says as her eyes drift shut. "No matter what—we've got this."

"No matter what," I agree, as I imagine what it would be like to just be happy.

Chapter Nine

TRISH

Layton truck pulls in the driveway and I run up and jump in the passenger side before he has a chance to get out and open my door.

"Good mornin', darlin'. You're in a good mood," he says taking me in. I'm in another band t-shirt and leggings, but today I left my hair down. I feel like it's gotten so much longer over the last couple months as it falls almost to my waist.

"Well, Claire doesn't hate me and we've had such an amazing week, I'm all caught up at work, and I feel like everything is working out," I say happily, practically bouncing in my seat. "Your mom was talking about you guys playing board games the other night, so I thought I would bring some over today," I explain as we look down at the absurdly large bag, stuffed full with games.

"Some, or the entire game closet?" he asks, shaking his head with a little smile on his face.

"I didn't know which ones to bring. Now that I think about it, she probably already has games there, huh?"

"My mom loves games, she'll be happy to have something different."

"Layton? I have no idea what I'm doing."

"What do you mean? You don't have to do anything, just hang out and talk," he tells me and turns towards his mom's house as anxiety washes over me.

"I know but, your mom is nothing like my mom. Your mom is so nice and fun. My mom is... serious. We never played games growing up. I don't know how to hang out with a fun mom." Layton reaches over, grabbing my hand, stopping my oversharing.

"You already did it. You spent hours the other night talking and laughing. Just do that. She is so excited to have you spend the day with her. Don't worry yourself about it," he says as he parks in his mom's driveway.

"I just want to make sure she has a good day. I'm not sure why I'm overthinking this so much," I say, playing with the duffle bag strap.

He reaches over and softly grabs my chin, turning me toward him. "Trish, you are enough. You don't have to be anything but yourself. I haven't seen my mom laugh like she did the other night in so long, and it looked effortless for you both. Don't try to be someone you're not—you're perfect just as you are." His eyes capture mine and I'm completely lost in his gaze. I fight the urge to lean into the feeling of his thumb tracing over my jaw, and I don't miss how his eyes track down to my lips.

It's obvious we are attracted to each other; I'd be an idiot not to admit that. He's a six foot-five cowboy, for God's sake. I'd also be an idiot to act on it, considering I don't know him and I'm in no way ready for a relationship after the shit-show with Brett.

"You should head inside before my mom comes out," he says though the words seem strained, and his eyes are still locked on my lips.

"I should," I whisper. My eyes flutter closed as he traces my bottom lip with the calloused pad of his thumb. I want him to kiss me. Hell, I really want him to pull out of this driveway, take me back home, and spend the day ruining my life—consequences be damned. Instead, he moves his hand away and settles himself back in his seat, seeming to shake the trance we were both caught in. "I'll be back at five to pick you up."

I take that as my cue to leave and let myself out of the truck before walking towards the house.

"Trish," he yells. I turn back to see his window rolled down. "What happened to letting me open your door?"

"I'm a big girl," I tell him.

He smiles back at me. "Can you just humor me and let me do it?"

"Fine," I pout like I'm annoyed before breaking out in a huge smile.

"Thank you for doing this," he says shifting into reverse. "You have no idea how much this helps me."

"I'm glad I can," I tell him as he smiles, letting the big dimples show in the corner of his mouth. "Now get to work before you get in trouble."

He laughs as he pulls out of the driveway, a smile still on his face. As I watch him disappear, I feel another piece of me breaking off. This time though, I realize the pieces breaking are the pieces of the Trish I created falling away—I can feel her falling apart. A part of me desperately wants to hold her together. She was safe. She didn't laugh too loudly, she didn't sing out of nowhere or dance without a care, and most of all, she made sure everyone liked her. Beneath those broken pieces of a woman, I feel the real me is desperately fighting to come out. I take a deep breath before walking to the door and knocking. There is some shuffling before the door opens, revealing Layton's mom on the other side with a light pink bandana, covered in smiley faces wrapped around her head.

"Trish, I'm so glad you came," she says, running out to wrap me in a hug. "Come in, I made snacks!"

She ushers me in, and the smell of cookies hits me as I cross the threshold.

"It smells amazing," I gush.

"I wanted to make you some stuff. This is the first break in treatments I've had in a while. I'm trying to make the most of it. I know once I go back on chemo, I won't be baking for a bit," she says as casually as if she were telling me about the weather.

"I'm so sorry, Ms. Kilier."

"Call me Ella and don't be sorry. We all go through things in life, this is just my thing," she tells me with a wave of her hand. "Plus, if my hair grew back too long, I wouldn't have an excuse to wear all these cute bandanas."

"Your bandana *is* adorable," I say honestly.

"I'll have to show you all of the ones I've got. Layton brings me home a new one at least once a week." She laughs. "I don't know how I got so lucky with that kid." She leads me into the living room where a tray of chocolate chip cookies and cinnamon rolls sits on the coffee table with two glasses of iced tea.

"This looks amazing," I tell her, my mouth watering at the delicious looking treats.

"Please eat up. In a few hours, I can make lunch. I figured for a girls' day we could cheat and have snacks first." I am instantly at peace. Layton was right, this is easy.

"You are a little carrot tree?" I say, tears streaking down my cheeks as I laugh hysterically.

We ended up picking a game where you have to put these plastic things in your mouth and read a card. Then the other person tries to guess what you're saying. We both suck, but I've never had more fun in my life.

"I'm not even going to ask," Layton says coming behind us.

We both look up at him as he takes us in. I can only imagine what we look like.

"Hurr haying ha hane," his mom says with the crazy contraption still in her mouth. Layton's eyebrows shoot up in confusion, which only makes us both laugh harder until we are both in an unstoppable fit of giggles.

"I'm just glad you guys are havin' fun," he says, his eyes locked on mine with an expression I can't quite name.

Ella climbs from the couch, taking the plastic piece and setting it in the bowl on the table. "Oh, honey, I had one of the best days I've had in my entire life," she says, taking my hands in hers. "Trish, I'm sure someone your age has a million other things they'd rather do than hang out here all day with an old lady like me, but I'm so thankful you did."

"I promise, I came today because I wanted to. And honestly, I really had an amazing day too."

"Well, I should let you kids get on the road. I'm exhausted; I think I'm going to go take a quick nap," she says, letting go of my hands before turning to Layton and patting him on the cheek.

"I will be back around nine with some dinner," Layton tells her, wrapping her in a hug.

He walks me out to the truck and opens the door so I can climb in. "Was it as scary as you thought?" he asks with a smirk on his face.

"No you were right; it was just like the other night. I love your mom, she's the nicest person I've ever met. She taught me how to make homemade mac and cheese for lunch. Then she showed me all of the bandanas you bought her."

I lock eyes back on Layton, who is just staring at me smiling.

"You had mac and cheese?" he asks, looking jealous.

"Don't worry, she saved you a bowl."

"Thank God. It's the best. At one point I had her making it once a week. She hasn't made it in so long, I figured she was mac'd out."

"I guess I should feel lucky I have the recipe right here then," I say, tapping on my head. "Unfortunately for you, I think my brain is mixing it with the cookie recipe."

"I've never met a girl like you."

I instantly feel the panic set in.

"Trish, why don't you act like a girl, for God's sake. It's embarrassing. My coworkers were there tonight, and you showed up without your hair and makeup done," Brett yells across the room. I hadn't even realized he was upset until the doors of the car shut and he pulled away.

"It was a picnic. I thought my outfit was nice," I say looking down at the shorts and top I picked.

"I'm fed up with you always holding yourself to shit standards. You made me look bad. I can't imagine what they thought of me being with someone like you," he yells, getting in my face. I shrink away. In the five years we've been together, he's never acted this way until recently—after he got a promotion at his dad's company.

"I'm sorry I upset you. I will get some nicer clothes," I tell him and instantly see the rage fade from his eyes. The man I love coming back to Earth.

"Thank you," he says softly, coming up to grab my face. I flinch out of instinct, but thankfully he misses it. "I'm sorry, baby, I just have so much more pressure on my shoulders now and you are a reflection of me."

"It's fine." My mind screams that this is anything but. He kisses my head before turning to walk away.

"Oh and, babe?" he says. "I forgot to tell you, I booked you a trip to the salon tomorrow at nine AM. She said plan to be there all day. I guess going blonde takes a while."

"What? I'm not going blonde. You know I love my hair," I argue, grabbing at the long red strands.

Instantly, I see the rage returning as he stalks toward me, and I step back.

"I really think you'd look much nicer as a blonde, Trish. You know how I love blondes." He twists a strand of the fiery red hair in his fingers with disgust written across his face as he looks at it. "No one likes being a redhead."

I feel a hand touch my arm and it breaks me from the past.

"Where'd you just go?" Layton asks with concern coating his words.

"I'm just tired. I think we should head home," I say softly, looking away.

I feel him hesitate, but he respects the boundary I've set and shuts the door before walking around to his side.

"Let's get you home."

The ride is completely silent. I feel him looking over at me every now and then, but my mind is filled. Is the girl I've been pretending to be worth being unhappy for? The other part of me—the part that is finally finding herself again—screams not to build the walls back up. I hate who I've been the last few years. I shuffle through these thoughts relentlessly until I hear the sound of a door shutting and realize we are back at the house. Layton is at my door, opening it for me.

"Can you at least tell me what I said that hurt you, so I can avoid doing this again?" he says quietly, blocking me from getting out of the truck.

I pause, debating if I should just tell or ignore the issue and go inside. Part of me wants to apologize for who I am and that I am not like most girls, but the bigger part of me says screw all of that.

"I know I'm not like most girls— I tried that and hated it." I hear the bite to my words and I mentally high-five myself as I jump from the truck and push past him.

"Trish," he says quietly behind me.

"Yeah?" I say twisting on my heels to face him as he closes the distance between us with slow, sure steps.

Part of me wants to back up, but instead I square my shoulders and hold my ground. I will not change for another man. This is me in all my chaotic glory—take it or leave it.

"When I said you are not like other girls, I meant that in a good way," he says with his hand coming up to my face. "I love that you don't wear makeup and dress how you want. Don't get me wrong, I have nothing against a girl that likes to do herself up, I just hate to see girls force themselves to. There ain't a damn thing wrong with being yourself."

His thumb brushes my cheek and I do the last thing I ever planned to. I shoot up on my toes and I kiss him. He wastes no time kissing me back, and before I know it, I'm hoisted up against him, my legs wrapped tightly around his waist as he walks us back until I'm pressed firmly against the door of the truck.

"Claire?" I say breathlessly between kisses.

"Is at the ranch with Tyler," he replies, understanding my question.

I lean back with a smirk on my face. "Did you plan this?"

"No, darlin', I didn't plan you getting pissed then kissin' the hell outta me," he says with a chuckle.

This is my chance to break apart. To go inside, take a freezing cold shower, and maybe put Buzz to use again. None of that is even half as appealing as the six-foot-five cowboy that I'm currently wrapped around. So, I lean in and kiss him again. He growls in approval and the kiss goes from hungry to damn-near desperate.

His big hands move under my shirt skimming over me, goosebumps break across my skin as a moan comes from my throat. We need to get into the house—now. Never in my life have I been so compelled to get a man undressed. I pull away as he drops me to the ground. I reach into my bag for the keys which seem impossible to find while he pulls the hair away from the one side of my neck and begins kissing his way up to my ear. I'm about to not even care and throw him down on the porch when my fingers finally brush the cool metal of the keychain. I quickly shove them in the door, and throw the door open as fast as I can. Twisting back to face him, he wastes no time hoisting me back into his arms slamming his lips back into mine, and kicking the door closed behind him.

I reach down, grabbing the hem of my shirt, breaking the kiss only to rip it over my head. His eyes go to the black satin bra and his gaze traces my body as I drop from his grip and take a few steps toward my room.

"I was gonna try to be a gentleman and leave this with the best damn kiss I've

ever had, but this is making that really difficult," he says. His voice is husky, and his eyes lock in on my chest as I unclasp my bra and let the material slide down my arms until it dangles from my fingers by one of the straps.

"Maybe I'm not looking for a gentleman right now," I tell him, hooking my thumbs in my legging and pushing them down my legs.

"Fuck," he growls, moving towards me, looking like a starved man and I'm his favorite meal. *I can't remember Brett ever looking so feral.* I force the thought of the him from my mind as I feel the heat of Layton's gaze as he looks down at me. "Where's your room darlin'?"

I point to the door and that's all he needs. His lips are back on mine, his hands skimming under my thighs to lift me into his arms as he carries me to my bed and lays me out in front of him. He stands back and stares at me deliberately. I fight the urge to cover myself.

He reaches behind him, ripping his shirt over his head in one movement before climbing up the bed between my knees. I reach down, unbuckling his jeans and using my feet to try and shove them down as I kiss him. His lips leave mine and travel down my neck and chest until his lips reach my breast. He softly kisses around my nipple, his eyes locked on mine as I watch him. He breaks from my stare as his whole mouth covers the sensitive peak. My back instantly bows from the bed as I moan with the contact.

He doesn't stop, instead he gently cups my other breast and rubs his thumb across my nipple, shooting another spark of electricity through me. *Is this what foreplay is? Because I think I'm a fan.*

Just when I feel like I am about to burst through the ceiling, he backs off and starts traveling down my stomach.

"Oh my God, I didn't shave," I say in a panic. "I didn't really plan for this to go this far, or I would have been prepared. I'm so sorry."

"Do you think not shaving is going to be a turn off for me?" he says with a smirk. "You could be full-seventies bush under these panties, and I would eat you like you were my first meal in days." His big hands wrap around my thighs, pulling me back toward him on the bed before hooking his fingers into the waistband of my panties and pulling them down my legs. He kisses his way back up until he's directly between my thighs—eyes once again locked on mine. "Any change of heart?" he asks.

"No," I say on a pant. The visual of him between my legs is enough to make me want to combust.

That's all the permission he needs to devour me. The world around me fades to a blur of colors as my muffled cries fill my ears. My fingers wrapped in his hair in a battle of shoving him away and holding him closer. His hands come up to hold my thighs as another wave crashes over me before the last one subsides.

His warmth leaves me as he shoves his pants down his hips off along with his boxers. I take in every inch of him as he slides on a condom. He's all man—hard and strong. My mouth waters as he climbs back over me, the solid length of him playing at my entrance. I can't help myself but to push myself closer, the friction pulling another moan from me.

He responds with a kiss. Our tongues battling against each other as he guides himself inside of me, releasing a low groan as he moves. I gasp, but he swallows my moans with his kiss. The whole situation is raw and frenzied, and I never want it to end. He switches from desperate, erratic thrusts to slow languid strokes that allow me to feel every single inch of him. That's all I need to fall over the edge into oblivion. And the sound of him following me keeps me there for longer than I've ever been before.

Chapter Ten

LAYTON

A month has passed since I slept with Trish. The entire drive to her house the next day, I tried to think of what the hell to say. My mom loves her. I come home every day to them giggling about something new. Hell, even Trish seems lighter the more time they spend together. If I let my inability to keep it in my pants ruin that, I would never forgive myself. I wasn't sure what to expect, but her running out with a huge smile and acting like nothing happened wasn't it at all.

I brought up my fear of it ruining everything and her response was that she wasn't really expecting more than that. I hadn't thought past wanting to touch her and I'll be damned if I haven't been fighting myself every day not to drag her back into her room.

"Layton?" Tyler says, getting in my face and waving his hands back and forth. "Dude, where are you? I've been yelling at you for like ten minutes."

"Shit, sorry. Mom had a rough night. I was up sitting outside of her door. I planned to sleep, but I was too worried I'd miss something," I tell him honestly.

"Why didn't you say something? You should have taken off. You know you can always take off."

"I know. Trish is there with her, now. Plus, there is too much going on here to miss any time if I don't need to."

"Trish? Claire's friend?"

"Yeah, she offered to hang out with her during the day." I pull my phone from my pocket for the hundredth time, checking to make sure I haven't missed a call or text.

Tyler rubs his jaw. I know he is about to send me home.

"I'm fine. Give me a job," I tell him.

"Okay, that baby cow you saved—Ohana—someone needs to feed him," he says, and I cock an eyebrow at him.

"My job is to feed a calf a bottle?" I ask.

"Yeah, man, maybe take a nap with him while you're at it," he says, patting me on the shoulder. "You have the world on your shoulders right now with your mom. I don't wanna see something happen to you because you forgot to take care of yourself. Promise you'll come to me if you need to talk."

I hang my head because I know myself well enough to know that's not a promise I can make. I find the small cow I saved last month curled in a ball in the corner of the stall. I make him a bottle and as soon as I open the door, his head pops up.

"So, Ohana, looks like I've been put on grunt duty today," I tell him. "Glad to see you looking healthier."

He shoves his head across my lap towards the bottle and I stick it in his mouth watching him gulp greedily before leaning my back against the wall.

"Rise and shine," Tyler's voice breaks through the darkness.

My eyes pop open and I see him leaning over the stall door. Ohana is running around the stall. The empty bottle is on the ground next to me.

"What time is it?" I ask deliriously.

"Five—time for you to go home," he says calmly.

"What!? You let me sleep for four hours." I yell jumping from the ground, my back screaming in protest for being in such an awkward position.

"Yes, I did. I don't regret that shit one bit, either."

"I'm so sorry, man. I—"

"Layton, I saw you here hours ago. I knew you'd be pissed, but I chose to let you sleep. You needed it. You have a lot going on. Now, go home," he says leaving no room for argument.

I leave the stall, softly patting Ohana on the way out.

"Thanks, man."

"Next time, call me and tell me what's going on. I got your back, always."

"I know you do," I tell him as we walk out of the barn towards my truck. "I'll see you tomorrow."

I jump in my truck and head to my mom's to get Trish. I hate to admit how much better I feel after that nap, but next time Tyler puts me on bottle-feeding duty, I will be setting an alarm—just in case.

Trish is already walking out the door as I pull into the driveway. My mom stands on the porch with a huge smile on her face as she laughs at whatever Trish says. She looks much better than she did yesterday, thank God. I jump from the truck, walking up to wrap her in a hug.

"A good day?" I ask as I hold her against me.

"Of course, it was. I taught Trish to make biscuits and gravy."

"My favorite," I say, smiling at Trish.

"I can't believe I went my entire life without having it," Trish says. "Can we stop at the store on the way back home? I'm going to try to make a dinner that didn't come from a can."

"Yeah, I gotta grab some stuff anyway," I say, kissing my mom on top of her head before following Trish to the truck. "I'll be back, mama."

"Thank you so much for today, Ella. I'll see you next week," Trish yells out the window as we pull away.

"I swear, I've only known your mom for like a month and she is already more of a mother than mine ever was. Is that a horrible thing to say?" she asks, still smiling ear to ear.

"Not if that's how you feel," I tell her.

"My parents just aren't good at affection, you know? We didn't hug or say I love you. They pushed academics. I think they looked at me more as someone to form into their dreams, instead of my own. It's not the job they wanted, but I did it anyway. They still resent me for that.

"How'd you get into cyber security?" I ask.

"My professor in college did a class on the side. He saw how well I was doing and said I should check it out. Day one, I knew I loved it. I really do have them to thank for me getting the job, though. If they they hadn't made me take all the classes they did, I would have never ended up here." She tells me. "How about you with the ranch?"

"I started helping Tyler out after his dad passed away. I realized quickly I'd never love doing anything like I love working on that ranch. I gotta bring you down there—it's heaven." I tell her as I pull into a parking spot in front of the grocery store.

"I would love that."

I smile at the thought as I jump from the truck and go around to open her door. "Meet you out here when you're done."

Chapter Eleven

TRISH

I weave through the aisles, filling my cart with everything I need for dinner tomorrow night.

I turn towards the stand that is normally stocked with fresh baked goods from Mrs. Emma, the owner. A nice gooey brownie is calling my name, but as soon as it comes into view, I realize it's empty.

"Sorry, honey, that darn cowboy just left with my whole display. If I'd known you were coming, I would have made him leave a brownie behind," Mrs. Emma says, coming up behind me.

"It's okay," I say, trying to hide the disappointment in my tone. *I really freaking wanted that brownie.* "Who needs that many snacks?"

She chuckles, "He's been coming in once a week for years and buying whatever I've got. He gives them to the workers on the ranch."

"Oh," I say, realizing it's Layton being nice.

"Next week, I'll make sure to save you one. How about this week, you take this on the house?" She walks to the cooler and grabs a half gallon of fudge-filled ice cream, placing it in my cart.

"Mrs. Emma, I can't take that. I mean, I will because it looks good, but I'm paying."

"Nonsense, dear. If you pay, there won't be a brownie here next week," she says, shooting me a stern look, that's almost comical on her sweet face.

"Fine," I say, accepting defeat. "Thank you. Really."

"I'm happy to do it. I remember how bad my cravings were. I would want the strangest things and when I couldn't get them, it would just ruin my day."

I know I am looking at her like she has ten heads, because her entire demeanor changes. For the first time since I met her, she looks uncomfortable.

"Well, honey, I should go check on the new cashier. Yesterday he gave someone a fifty instead of a twenty. Sweet kid though." She doesn't give me a chance to respond and scurries away, leaving my mind racing. I pull out my phone, scrolling through my calendar. The edges of my vision blurring as I try to place my last period.

I've been sick since before we moved. I figured it was just the stress finally catching up to me.

I walk on autopilot until I'm face to face with the dreaded boxes, staring at them like they are the most vile things to exist. The nausea I thought I had all but tackled slams into me full force as the world spins around me.

I'm going to pass out. There is nothing I can do to stop it. I reach forward trying to grab anything as the music over the speakers muffles in my ears.

"Woah, you good?" A voice calls, but it's too far away as I feel myself swaying. Thundering steps approach but the world around me fades to black. My knees buckle just as strong arms wrap around me.

"Trish, what's going on?"

I know that voice.

I peek up through the tears at the last face I wanted to see right now. His face is full of worry as he looks me over. He stops for only a second to look at the box still clutched tightly in my hands. If it bothers him, he's got one helluva poker face.

"You're okay. Let's get you outside and get some fresh air. He grabs the test from my hands, tossing it into the cart before shoving it to the side of the aisle and leading me out. Once he has me seated on the bench, he squats down in front of me.

"I'm so sorry," I rush out, my mind is racing with how horrible this situation actually is.

His hands cup both sides of my face, pulling it up so I can look at him.

"Trish, why are you sorry?"

"I think I'm pregnant," I deadpan.

"I kinda figured that part out," he says softly.

"It wouldn't be yours," I rush out, realizing he must think I'm truly insane. It's only been a month since we hooked up, and here I sit almost fainting with a pregnancy test in hand.

"I figured that too. But if it was, we would figure it out."

I let out a laugh. "God, I'd so much rather it be yours." His eyebrows pull together and I realize I am making this situation so much worse. "Ignore that. That was extremely weird. I'm sorry." I drop my head back into my hands.

"You know my ex and I tried for years to have a baby. Didn't happen. I thanked God for that when I saw his true colors. Then I escape, and this is what I get."

His face completely changes from sweet understanding to unabated rage before my eyes. For the first time, his bear-like size seems intimidating.

"What do you mean, you escaped?" The tone in his voice is like pure ice. I look at his eyes, but all the warmth and comfort has left them.

I realize I've said too much and I freeze, shooting my eyes to the ground. There is complete silence for what feels like minutes, though I'm sure it's only a few seconds when he stands up abruptly.

"Let's get you in the truck. I'll be right out," he says helping me to my feet and getting me settled, before storming back into the store. I sit in the passenger seat, watching him reach the glass doors in complete shock at how badly that all just went.

A woman about to walk in stops, looking him up and down—not a care in the world that he looks as if he could destroy the world with his anger—before combing her fingers through her golden locks and sauntering after him. She's at least double his age, but I can't blame her at all. He is gorgeous.

What the hell am I going to do?

I know I haven't even taken the test yet. Hell, maybe it is stress and there isn't a life growing inside of me. I put my hand over my still-flat stomach. I imagine what Brett would do if he somehow found out. The images of him over me that night play in my head. *Would he kill me?* The longer I'm away from him, the more I realize how many red flags I ignored.

The night he was drunk he whispered in my ear that I'd never be anyone else's. That he would never let me go, and if he ever thought I was going to leave, he would find a way to make me stay. That night I looked at him in a way I never had before, but the next day he was normal, and I brushed it off as him trying to be sweet and his drunk brain taking it too far.

The sudden sound of the door opening makes me jump.

"It's just me, sorry. Your groceries are in the back. Let's get you home."

My eyes shoot to the bed of the truck. Sure enough, there are bags filling it.

"You didn't have to do that."

"I know, but you planned an entire dinner for tomorrow. I wanted to make sure you had it all so I called mom to make sure. I grabbed the last few things."

I quickly reach for my purse to hand him some money.

"I got it," he says, softly grabbing my wrist.

I look up at him.

"Layton, you don't have to do that."

"Darlin', there were like ten things in the cart and if I didn't want to do it, I wouldn't have," he states simply.

"Thank you," I say, too weak to argue, but when he isn't looking, I slide the hundred-dollar bill in his center console. As much as I appreciate the gesture, I can take care of myself.

"I'm sorry for how I acted back there. I didn't mean to scare you," he says, breaking the silence that has taken over the cab.

"You didn't scare me," I say quietly.

"I saw you flinch. I shouldn't have gotten like that. Just the thought of you having to *escape* someone pisses me off."

"Brett and I were together for seven years. I thought I was in love with him. I honestly don't know if he changed, or if I finally just woke up. The more I look back on our life together, the more things I see that I missed," I say. "I'm sorry, I'm not sure why I'm over sharing again. You have enough to worry about."

Currently, I'm going on Mrs. Emma's assumptions and a million other symptoms I want to pretend I haven't had. I ran to be *free*. But that stupid little white box in the truck bed could destroy that for me.

"Trish?" Layton's voice pulls me from my internal crisis. My eyes shoot over, locking on his before they trail behind him to see we have made it to the house.

"Sorry, just thinking about what to make for dinner." I say.

"You head inside, I'll bring your things in."

I go to argue, but I am met with a stern look, and decide against it.

As soon as I hit the door, nausea rolls through me. Not the kind that has me running to throw up, but the kind that makes me want to crash to the floor in a heap and never get up again. I don't even know how to feel. Part of me feels like this is some kind of cruel cosmic joke. There was a time years ago, I would have killed to have a baby with Brett. We actually talked about it and tried for a year, but nothing happened. I decided that it wasn't the right time, and we went back to life as normal.

Now I sit here contemplating if my life is ruined by the same baby I prayed for just a few years ago.

Layton walks in, placing all my things on the counter in one trip.

"Will you be okay if I head out or do you need me to stay?" he asks, his words sounding wary.

"You can leave, I've got this," I lie.

I know he doesn't believe me, but it also isn't his place to question my choice.

"Whatever happens, you are going to get through it," he says with a sad smile as he walks out my front door.

As soon as his truck pulls out of the driveway I rush to the bag, pulling out the box, unable to take the suspense a second longer. I hesitate a second before walking to the bathroom and ripping the box open. Peeing on the end, then I cap it and place it on the counter before setting a timer and saying a little prayer. The alarm goes off, and I flip the stick in my hand—two solid bright pink lines staring back at me.

"No!" I yell, tossing the test across the room, watching it hit the wall and fall to the floor. "Why would you let this happen to me? Why would you let me get free just to trap me again?" I scream as tears pour uncontrollably from my eyes as I collapse on the cold floor.

I hear a knock at the bathroom door.

"Trish," Layton's voice sounds through the wood. "You left your wallet in the car. I heard you screaming, and I let myself in. Please just tell me you're okay. If you want me to leave I will, but I don't want to leave if you're not okay."

"I'm fine," I choke out.

Silence stretches out for a few moments, and I think maybe he left.

"Trish, can I please come in?" he says quietly, like he's questioning if he should even be asking at all.

"Yes." Maybe I simply don't want to be alone to process the fact that I will never be free. Maybe part of me wants to just pretend it isn't as bad as it is. Whatever the reason... I let him in.

The second the door flies open and Layton's eyes lock on mine, I lose it.

"It's going to be okay," he says dropping down and pulling me into his arms.

"It's *not* going to be okay," I say, sounding harsher than I should. He doesn't even have to be here, let alone be supporting me through something that's completely not his problem. "He's going to come after me. I can't let him near this baby. What if he hurts them too?"

I hear a growl from the back of his throat above me and realize I admitted something I've only told Claire. My eyes fly up to lock on his, and I see rage burn through his chestnut eyes.

"Excuse me?" he says. A hint of danger wrapped in his words.

"Nothing. I'm just panicking. I shouldn't be telling you this," I say, pulling myself off of the ground before going to walk past him.

He reaches out, gently grabbing my arm to stop me in my tracks. Basically pinning me into the door frame with him.

"He hurt you?" he asks, his voice soft, though I can tell it's forced.

"I—" I should lie but I already know he won't believe me if I do. "He did." I pause trying to find the words to explain the mess inside my head. "It only happened once."

Layton stays silent, and I yank my eyes down to the ground.

"I'm okay though, I swear. I got away. I'm here. I survived, and I haven't heard a word from him since I left."

I look up at him again, but now he is locked in on the wall behind me. His jaw clenched so tightly it looks as if it could break. For a second, I debate fearing him. He's huge, at least double my size, but the fear doesn't hit me.

"Do you have anything to protect yourself?" he asks, breaking the tense silence.

"Oh, I do!" I say, rushing out of his hold towards the front door where I grab the metal baseball bat we keep there.

"That's your protection?" he asks.

"Yup."

He just shakes his head at the metal bat in my hands as if he's sad for me, and I hate that.

"I'm a lot stronger than I look. I can protect myself."

"I'm not worried about if you can handle yourself, Trish. I'm worried you just told me someone hurt you. Your face was filled with what seems a hell of a lot like terror. My mind is racing with what that asshole did."

"Layton, this isn't your problem. I can take care of myself," I say to him, a bite to my words. "You've only known me for like a month."

"I don't have to know you to want to kill him. He hurt you. He put his hands on a woman and clearly made her feel unsafe. Made her feel like she had to escape to find freedom. I don't care if I just met you five seconds ago, I would react the exact same way. I want to hurt *him*."

I stand staring at him as he paces back and forth taking up a huge chunk of my small kitchen. He looks menacing, but I only fear for Brett.

"Okay, I get that, but please don't do anything stupid. Like I said, I haven't heard a word from him since I left. I doubt he's even looking for me.

He cocks one eyebrow at me.

"Just promise me you're being safe. I have no idea what you've been through, but I can't imagine someone not caring about you leaving."

"I'll be okay," I tell him again.

"Yet that look on your face said anything but. I know I'm overstepping, but I'm freaked the hell out—I'm not gonna lie," he says before walking toward the front door looking like he wants to do anything but leave.

As he does, the sense of security he brought goes with him.

A knock pulls me from my sleep. I look at my phone through dreary eyes realizing it's already twelve. Another knock raps on the door. This one a bit more aggressive than the last.

I slip out of bed, walking down the steps and rubbing my eyes as I pull open the front door. Layton stands there in his worn jeans, a dirt-stained t-shirt, and a cowboy hat. His eyes trail down the front of me before I realize that I am still in no more than an oversized t-shirt myself. His eyes slowly trail back up until they lock on mine.

"Darlin', do you always answer the door without pants on?" he asks me his voice husky.

"Normally no, but I was asleep."

"It's noon," he states plainly.

"I couldn't sleep," I say, moving so he can enter.

He huffs out a breath as he rubs a hand across the scruff of his beard. "I need to apologize about how I acted last night. I was pretty riled up when I left here. I should have thought before I spoke and got you more upset," he tells me. "I brought you something. You don't have to take it if you don't want it, but I'd really prefer you did."

He holds up a black box I didn't even realize he was carrying.

"What is that?" I question.

"A gun."

"Layton, I don't need a gun," I tell him looking at the box like it's going to attack me.

"I want to teach you how to use it. Trish, I know damn well that look on your face. You're scared he is going to find you. I won't pry and ask you what that asshole did, but just keep it. You don't ever have to use it if you don't need to, but I could teach you how to shoot. I could get you your license to carry and a holster. You could protect yourself."

"I don't know."

"Think about it for your baby, then?" he says, almost as if he's begging me.

I stare at the box in his hands, realizing he's right—this isn't just about me anymore. My mind argues Brett would never kill me, but I also know that's a lie because he almost did once. I'd be a fool to think he's not capable of worse.

"Can I think about it, at least? Guns scare me. They kill people."

"Yeah, that's kind of the point," he says. "Of course, you can think about it."

He puts the box on the counter, his eyes once again scanning down my body. I can't imagine how I look right now. On reflex, I reach up, running my fingers through my chaotic sleep hair.

"I'm sorry I look a mess," I say.

He steps forward until there is no room between us and runs his hand down the side of my face. "Never apologize for how you look. You look hot as hell right now. I've wanted you again every day since the first time, but I'm trying like hell to respect whatever wall you built since then."

I waste no time overthinking it and slam my lips against his, letting him carry me to my room and help me forget the chaos that my life has once again become. I want my hands on every inch of his body. I've spent the last month holding myself back. If I'm being at all honest with myself, whatever it is we are doing is the last thing I need, but as he pushes me over the edge and the colors dance through my mind—I can't find it in me to care. *We're both adults, chasing release, that's all this is*, I lie to myself.

His fingers trace lazy lines up and down my sides as I lay cradled against his strong chest. He freezes when he hits a raised scar on my back. I was so grateful the other night when it didn't come up, but tonight I tell him the entire story. He holds me as I spill every secret and soak his bare chest with tears. He never stops me, only pulls me in tighter as the words fall from my lips. I ask myself over and over why I am spilling my guts to this man. Maybe it's because he's huge and I feel safer than I've ever felt. Maybe it's because I've just held it all in so damn long and I've finally broken, and it just so happens he's here to witness the mess.

Whatever the reason, I feel lighter than I have in years once I have it all out. I can't imagine what Layton is thinking. This is probably way more than he thought he was signing up for. He just was being nice and now he has a naked pregnant woman airing all her dirty laundry after sex. I cringe at myself reaching up to wipe some of the tears from my eyes. I don't think this could get any worse.

Chapter Twelve

LAYTON

I ended up staying the night with Trish. After she broke down and told me the story about her piece-of-shit ex leaving her to die, I couldn't leave. I called my mom's neighbor to see if she could go spend the night with her.

I laid the entire night with her wrapped in my arms, sleeping softly against my chest with my eyes glued to the ceiling, asking myself what the hell I've gotten myself into and why the hell am I still here instead of running. The answer is that the thought of anything happening to her makes me crazy. I know she is having a baby with another man, but for some reason I'm having a hell of a hard time giving a shit. In my mind, that asshole doesn't exist.

She's drawn a deep line in the sand that she wants nothing more than being friends that sometimes end up in bed together. The problem is, I don't know how long I can be okay with just being Trish's friend.

"I'm just about to pull out some lunch if you want some," Luke says, coming up behind me in his wheelchair as I grab my fifth cup of coffee of the day from Tyler's kitchen. He opens the oven and I'm hit with an amazing smell.

"I just ate, but you know I can't turn down anything you make." He cuts a square and puts a plate of lasagna in front of me. I take a huge bite and it burns the roof of my mouth, but I don't even care—the kid has skills. I look up to see him staring out the window with a sad look on his face. I follow his eyes to Mia talking to Derek.

"You okay?"

"Sometimes I wonder if I'll get a chance to find someone. Don't tell anyone I said that. I've accepted my life for what it is. It's just not as easy to meet people."

"It'll happen," I reassure him.

"I hope so. Tyler looks so happy lately, now Derek walks around here smiling all day."

"Tyler told me you are moving out? That should give you some more freedom. You could make a dating thing online. You never know."

"Can't hurt," he agrees as he pours himself a cup of coffee.

"I can't believe he's not freaking the hell out," I tell him.

"I'm so glad he met Claire. Is it just me or is he a lot less of an asshole lately?"

"Oh, he's a lot less of an asshole," I agree. "I'm happy for you, man," I say, getting up to wash my already empty plate. "I'm sure the guys will miss your cooking around here, though."

"I'll come by sometimes just so they don't wither away from Tyler's cheese sandwiches."

"Oh God, don't remind me," I say, feeling the slight gag as I think back. Luke was sick, so Tyler tried to be nice and make everyone lunch. He made cheese sandwiches but couldn't find cheese, so he used cottage cheese and mayo on white bread.

Luke has tears streaming down his face watching my face twist in disgust. "I can't believe you tried to eat that thing."

"I was trying not to be an asshole," I tell him as I walk out the door.

"Layton, you're always an asshole," he calls after me. "Send the guys in to eat, would ya?"

"I will. Thanks, Luke!"

I walk through the field heading to Tyler. When I get to his side, I realize he's staring at something.

"What is that thing?" I ask, staring at the poor duck in front of me that looks like it went toe to toe with Mike Tyson.

"That's Hen," Tyler says matter-of-factly.

"It's a duck."

"Yeah."

"Why the hell did you name it Hen?" I ask.

"Because it's a cute name, and I named her," Mia says coming up behind me with a huge smile across her face.

"You know a hen is a chicken, right?" I ask her, still looking at the poor beat up duck she is walking over to with a hose in one hand and a blue plastic pool in the other.

"Yup, A hen beat her up, can you believe it? So, I named her Hen, so she gains more confidence to fight back." She throws the pool onto the ground next to the duck, unkinking the end of the hose towards the pool and watching it fill. "See, girl? Now you get your very own pool."

I run my hand through the scruff on my face and I contemplate if that makes any sense before accepting Mia could name a duck *Dog* and I wouldn't argue with her.

"Does she need to go to the vet? I can run her over there," I say.

"I looked her over really good. She just lost feathers and hurt her pride," Tyler answers.

At that moment, Hen locks onto me like she just processed she was supposed to defend herself and takes off towards me.

"What the hell!?" I say as I go to step backwards the duck flies up at my legs, doing her best to take me down. I reach down, fighting through the attack. "Alright, Hen, point proven. You're a badass, but take it out on the chickens next time, you lunatic," I say, finally wrapping the angry thing in my hands before I walk her over and set her in the half-full pool.

Mia has tears streaming down her cheeks as she cracks up.

"See, Hen, I knew you had it in you!" I can't help but laugh with her.

Mia has only been around a couple of months. She has had it rough. Her parents kicked her out the day she turned eighteen, but Tyler's mom offered her to let her live with her. Knowing the hell she's been through and seeing her light this whole damn farm up with a smile every day is just proof she's the strongest damn kid I've ever met.

The sound of my phone ringing cuts through Mia's laughter, and I pull it from my pocket seeing Trish's name lighting up the screen.

"Hey, you okay?" I ask as I quickly answer.

"I want to learn to shoot," she says, but her voice sounds off, and I instantly panic.

"Okay, I'll head over there now and pick you up," I tell her. "Did something happen?"

The line goes silent.

"Trish?" I say.

"I don't know, I'm probably overreacting," she says softly.

"What is it?" I ask, and Tyler looks at me with concern, but I ignore him.

"Today, at the store, I swore I saw him. I could be losing my mind, but it looked just like him, but then he was gone."

I start walking towards my truck without another word, phone pressed against my ear and the world fading out around me.

"You good?" I hear Tyler yell behind me.

"I gotta go," I yell back.

"Is it your mom?" he asks.

"No." Thats all I say before jumping in the truck and peel out of the driveway. "Talk to me, Trish"

Again, I'm met with silence. My mind is racing.

"Darlin', please," I beg.

"It was probably no one, but I'm scared and I don't know what else to do."

"I'll be there in ten."

Five minutes later, I'm pulling into my mom's driveway. Before I can jump out of the truck, she walks out of the front door in a pair of skin-tight black leggings and an oversized band t-shirt. Her red hair is pulled in a ponytail, and she looks hot as hell. I jump out, beating her to opening the passenger door.

"Thank you," she says with a sad smile as she climbs up into her seat. "I feel bad leaving her early."

"I called Evelyn, she'll be here soon. She told me today was a good day. Is she lying?"

"Today is the best day she's had all week. I'm so sorry to make you come get me for this. I don't even know if this is a good idea. I know I'm safe, but then a part of me keeps saying I'm not crazy. If something happened to Claire or the baby because I didn't at least try to protect us, I could never forgive myself." I put my hand on Trish's, which instantly stops her rambling and causes her to look over at me.

"You never have to use it if you don't need it, but at least this way you will know what you're doing," I reassure her and see her shoulders visibly relax. "If any point you change your mind, we pack up and leave. Deal?"

"Deal," she says.

She looks over, her eyes locking on my hand on top of hers and then slowly up to my eyes. She's a whole lot of something, and I know I'm already in way too deep. I want to track her ex down and scream that she's mine.

"There are a lot of monsters out there darlin'. Can't hurt to be safe," I say taking my hand off of hers before shifting the truck in reverse.

"You're right," she says, reaching into her bag. "Your mom went with me today." She hands me a black and white photo. I know it's an ultrasound, but I've got no idea what I'm actually looking at. All I know is that I can feel myself smiling.

"You're gonna have to walk me through this," I say, looking into her eyes to see they're lit up with excitement.

"I'm already fourteen weeks. That's the little face. The doctor said she looks healthy," she says, her eyes tearing up as she points to what I can now make out as eyes and a nose. "I got bloodwork done today, so I'll know if I'm having a little boy or a little girl by next week."

"She?" I ask her as she stares teary eyed at the photo.

"They are ninety-five percent sure. I got labs done to verify, but the tech was very sure she was right." I can't help but smiling picturing a mini-Trish running around in giant random t-shirts of bands I've never heard of with fiery red hair.

I pull out to the road watching her nervously twist her hands in her lap.

"You know you can back out at any time. No matter how I feel, this is your choice fully," I reassure her.

"I know, but something in my gut is telling me I need to do this. If I'm being honest with you, I'm terrified."

"If I'm being honest, you should have some fear. You are about to be in charge of a weapon that can kill people. I have a safe in the back for you to keep it in, and I will teach you gun safety at the range. When that little nugget comes, you have to know where this is at all times. It is fully your responsibility," I tell her, knowing it may sound harsh, but the reality of not taking care of it is even harsher.

"Okay, I can do this," she says to herself.

"I know you can," I tell her because even though I barely know her, I can tell she's a fighter. I just wish I could trust her when she says she's not in danger.

We pull into the range and Trish is still staring out the window.

"The scariest part to me is what if I have to use it? What if I'm not safe, you know?" she says turning her eyes back to mine. "It's been months, and nothing has happened, but part of me feels like I'm one second away from it all being ripped apart. Just like before."

"I hope you know that if it ever comes to that, you made the right choice. At the end of the day, it's you or him."

"I loved him," she says the words so softly I barely catch them, but my heart breaks for her. I can't imagine loving someone and fearing them at the same time.

"I know you did," I tell her, jumping from the truck and quickly walking to her side to open her door.

"I don't ever want to put you in a position where you aren't comfortable. If you are only doing this because you feel pressured, we'll leave. I just want you to be safe. Hell, I'll camp on the porch while you guys sleep, if you want me too."

"You are not sleeping on the porch," she laughs. "I'm a big girl. I can make my own choices. I promise, I want to learn. It's just not something I thought I'd ever have to learn."

Chapter Thirteen
TRISH

"You do realize if I ever actually need to use this thing, I won't have any of this extra crap, right?" I probably yell, since I can barely hear anything.

I'm currently holding a pistol facing a silhouette of a man that I'm supposed to fill with bullets, I have these massive clear glasses on and these giant earmuff things. I feel absurd.

"What?" I say trying to make out what he's saying behind me.

I'm just about to rip them off when I feel his body come up behind mine. The right side of the earmuffs are lifted from my head and replaced with his mouth.

"I said, you won't be shooting a hundred times. You should only have to shoot once." His voice whispers in my ear and I instantly clench my thighs together. "You gotta keep your legs shoulder width apart." Again, a whisper.

I say nothing, just follow what he says as he snakes a knee between my thighs and inches them apart.

"Now, lift the gun, aim, and pull the trigger slowly as you exhale." With that, he sets the covering back over my ear and steps away, leaving me cold and so unfocused it's not even funny. I do what he says, though. I don't imagine Brett. I picture the asshole that stole my purse from my shoulder back in New York, then knocked that poor old woman over trying to get away. *Screw that guy.*

I pull the trigger then shut my eyes. I'm too afraid to look and see that I blew it. I hear Layton behind me, but I have no clue what he's saying. His warmth returns and he slowly grabs the gun from my still aiming arms. I twist to face him, lifting the earmuffs from my ears.

"Not bad, darlin'," he says.

I open my eyes and look back over my shoulder to see the shot is low and left of where I was aiming but I still hit it, which is shocking.

"I can't believe I just shot a gun," I say.

"Next time, let's just practice keeping those pretty eyes open, okay?" he says, his face inches away from mine. I lean up and kiss him, it's not drawn out, but it still shoots little tingles through me. When I pull back, he is looking at me like he wants to toss me over the bench in front of everyone here and have his way with me.

"Can I try again now?" I ask softly breaking the moment, so I don't let him drag me out of here like a cave man.

"Absolutely."

"Do you have anywhere you need to be tonight?" Layton asks as we head home.

"Nope."

Shooting wasn't as scary as I thought it would be, but the thought of needing a gun makes me nauseous. I really hope I'm being dramatic. Today after the ultrasound, I swore I saw him. It was only a second and he wasn't dressed like he normally would be, but the face was him.

"Do you want to go to the ranch? It's almost sunset," he asks.

"Yes!" I say. "I've been so jealous of Claire getting to go there, it sounds magical."

He pulls down a dirt road with a huge sign over the entrance that says *Magnolia Falls Ranch*. The further we get down the road, the more I feel like I am on another planet. Fields surround us full of animals grazing on the green grass. The sunlight makes the plants look like they're dancing as the wind blows across the fields. Every inch of the property is drenched in natural beauty. He pulls up next to another lifted truck and hops out walking to my side to let me out.

"I didn't think you'd be back today," A man that I recognize from the bar a few months ago says.

"Tyler, this is Trish. Trish, this is my best friend, Tyler." Layton introduces us as he helps me from the truck. "We're gonna go watch the sunset. Figured I could show her around."

"Yeah, man, the guys all just wrapped up for the night and headed out. You got the ranch to yourself," he says, climbing into his truck. "Trish, it was nice to meet you again."

"You ready?" Layton asks, grabbing my hand and leading me towards the barn. "The back of the barn is going to have to do for today since we have ten minutes, but I know someone that will make it even better than any other spot."

We walk inside to a stall that seems empty and then I see him standing in the back corner. A small black and white cow who I'm assuming is Ohana.

"He is so much cuter than I could have imagined," I say.

"Let's bring him out with us." He opens the doors and leads the small cow towards the back into a fenced in area. Ohana takes off, awkwardly running through the dirt. Behind him is a scene unlike anything I've ever experienced. The fields go for miles until they hit the horizon which is painted in pastels over the distant mountains. The sun slowly sinks behind them sending the sky shifting to pink and orange. I'm speechless. Layton comes up behind me, wrapping his arms around my shoulders, and I can't help but sink into him. I realize this is way beyond a casual hook up. I realize I'm falling in love with this man. That scares the shit out of me, but at the same time, in the seven years I was with Brett, I didn't feel half as comfortable as I do with Layton in the few months I've known him.

I twist toward, him looking up into his eyes because as amazing as the view is behind me—looking at him is better.

"Why are you still here?" I ask him.

"What do you mean?"

"Why are you still spending time with me? I'm a disaster. I've been so overwhelmed by life, I haven't done my makeup or hair in months, and I wear basically a uniform of oversized old band t-shirts and black leggings."

He twists me toward the barn, pinning me against it. "You are yourself. You are caring and strong. I don't give a shit about you having fancy hair, makeup, or clothes. You are, honest to God, the most beautiful woman I've ever met. I like this," he says tracing down to my heart.

"And I'm pregnant by a man that may or may not want to hurt me. Don't you think that's a bit much to add to your already full plate?"

"I thought about all of that, and I can't really find it in me to give a shit about it being too much or too little. I like you. That includes whatever baggage you have. Give me that shit, and I'll carry it. I know you think you need to carry it all yourself, but you don't."

"I'm scared to give you more than this," I tell him honestly. "I think I might be broken."

"You are not broken. You *won*. You are healing from something no one should ever have to heal from," he says, tracing his fingers down my cheek and wiping away a tear that's slipped free. I hate that he makes it so easy to cry. I've always hated showing emotions in front of anyone. I honestly can't tell you a time I cried in front of another person before Michael's funeral. I blame the hormones.

"I may never be able to fully give myself to you," I tell him, wanting him to understand the gravity of our situation... Trying to give him a way out.

"I know," he says. "I still stand by what I said."

I lean in and he follows, pinning me deeper into the wood of the barn wall. We kiss like the world is on fire and we are about to burn down with it. I kiss him until I feel like my lungs are burning from lack of oxygen. It's still not enough. I crave him more than anything in my life, and it is terrifying. I know I can do this by myself, but something about him is peaceful. It's like the second he's near me, I don't have to pretend. How you can feel more you with another person than you do alone is unfathomable to me, but with him—I do.

A phone ringing breaks us apart. He pulls his phone from his pocket, and I see Evelyn's name lighting the screen. Layton's face drops as he quickly answers it.

"Hello?" His voice is already panicked. "We will be right there." I waste no time figuring out what happened and run over to the tiny calf and do my best to coax him towards the barn. Thankfully, he sees me and runs towards me nudging me with his nose. "Come on Ohana. Let's get you back to bed, buddy.

"She's sick again. Evelyn isn't strong enough to help her to the shower." I see the war in his eyes and the pain that is ripping through him.

"Let's go get her," I say as Ohana walks into his stall and Layton latches the door.

"I can drop you off on the way," he says.

I touch his shoulder making him look down at me. This huge bear of a man is trying his best to save his mom from something he has absolutely no control over... I hate that I'm adding more to his plate.

"I want to help." He quietly shakes his head while grabbing my hand and leading me to the truck. I climb in, and he wordlessly closes the door.

Chapter Fourteen

LAYTON

Trish wastes no time when we get to the house. She jumps from the truck, throwing open the door to the house, and running up the steps to my mom's room, taking them two at a time as I follow behind. As soon as she walks in the door, she's at my mom's side, who's covered in puke and pets her hair out of her face.

"Hey," she says sweetly.

"Trish, baby girl, you are back," my mom says weakly. "My good day ended."

"I know, I'm sorry," she says. I stare at her and can't help but smile. She's so wrong, I couldn't replace this.

I couldn't find someone that cares about my mom like she does.

I quickly thank Evelyn for sitting with her and reassure her that she is a huge help as I take in Trish talking to my mom as if she were her own.

"Layton, baby, is that you?"

I walk over to her, dropping down next to her. "Yeah, mama, I'm here too. Let's get you to the bathroom, okay?"

She smiles up at me, letting me wrap my arms around her to carry her down the hall. Trish is in front of us opening the door.

"I'm sorry I ruined your night, guys," she says. "Nonsense," Trish says. "We were already on our way back here." I sit my mom on the closed lid of the toilet. I don't remember her ever being this weak and it kills me.

"Did you have a good date?" she asks.

"We did, he brought me to watch the sunset at the ranch. I got to meet a baby cow."

"That ranch is just amazing, isn't it?" my mom says. "Layton meeting Tyler was the best thing that happened to him. You wouldn't believe it, but my sweet boy was a bit of a wild child for a bit there."

Trish puts her hand to heart in fake shock. "You're kidding?"

My mom laughs weakly. "The school called me once, when he just started high school. They caught him sneaking behind the bleachers with a senior girl. I guess he had convinced all the kids he'd transferred from another school and was a senior. I'm sure it wasn't hard to believe since he went into freshman year already over six feet tall and with a full beard. I thought them finding out he was a freshman would slow it down, but those girls were obsessed."

"I can't blame them." Trish laughs as she grabs my mom's shirt and throwing it into the hallway.

"I knew right then and there I had my hands full with him being a ladies' man. It was like a revolving door of girls for years. Not even Tyler could break his Casanova ways."

"I wasn't that bad," I defend myself.

"Layton, you brought three girls to prom," she says, making Trish burst out laughing.

"They were fine with it."

"Like I said—Casanova. Then I got sick and there wasn't another girl over until you. Seeing you walk up that day was the best thing I've seen in a long time. I haven't seen Layton smiling like that in years."

"Let's get you cleaned up." I tell her once she's down to her underwear and bra. I look at Trish realizing she has been in here just helping me get my mom ready to get in the bath. She hasn't said a word. Just jumped into action to help. I have become so numb to this whole thing. The last time she was doing chemo I had no choice but to step up and help her shower.

There are some things in life you don't get a chance to give a second thought. This is one of those things. I'll be damned if I ever let my mom sit in her own filth because I'm too proud to wash her. This woman wiped my ass, bathed me, and cared for me. The least I can do is take care of her back.

"I'm going to let you finish up here and go get her bed remade. Where can I find new bedding?"

"In her closet, top shelf," I tell her as she turns to walk out but I catch her hand as she goes. "Thank you."

"Of course." The smile she gives me floods my chest with a warmth I've never felt before and I don't know what to do with.

"I've never seen you look at anyone like you look at her," my mom says as I help her to the tub.

"That's because I've never met anyone like her."

"I will go throw that in the wash in a second." Trish tells me folding down the blankets on the freshly made bed as I carry my mother in.

"I got it. You've already done more than enough," I say as I lay my mom in her bed tucking her into the covers. As I go to pull away, she touches my face.

"Baby, I was so scared you wouldn't fall in love because of me. I just want you to know, I think Trish is the most amazing woman I have ever met. I love her. I'm so happy you won't be alone when I'm gone. I just really hope I'm here to meet that sweet baby of yours," she whispers as she drifts to sleep leaving me and Trish completely silent.

"Oh, my God," I hear Trish whisper behind me. I quickly pull her from my mom's room, softly shutting the door behind us and leading us down the hall to my old room where I've been sleeping. "She thinks the baby is yours, Layton. I promise, I will tell her the truth tomorrow," she says pacing back and forth frantically.

"Hey," I say, grabbing her shoulders to stop her panic. "It's okay. Last time mom was on chemo she struggled with her memory, it's fine."

"Layton, it's going to break her heart. I feel terrible."

"It's going to be okay; we'll figure it out. Go get a shower in my bathroom. I will toss the laundry in and hop in downstairs, then we can talk okay. I can bring you home if you want."

She looks like she wants to argue but looks at both our outfits and wrinkles her nose.

"Can I stay?" she asks softly.

"I was hoping you would," I tell her as I open my drawer, pulling out a t-shirt and boxers and tossing them to her as she disappears into the bathroom.

I walk down the hall scooping up the dirty sheets from the floor, my mind is racing to the point where I don't even realize I've made it to the laundry room and started a load.

By the time I've showered and made it back to my bedroom, I've made up my mind. Seeing Trish laid across my bed in my t-shirt asleep with her hand protectively over her belly only engrains the idea deeper in my mind.

I grab a blanket from the closet and climb into bed next to her, covering us both.

"Hey," she says twisting towards me. "I'm sorry, I didn't mean to fall asleep."

I bring my hand up, softly running my fingers through her hair as I push it away from her face.

"She's the size of an avocado," she says, exhaustion coating her words as her blue eyes fall closed. "I hope I'm as good of a mom as yours."

"You are going to be an amazing mom.," I reassure her.

"I'm terrified he is going to find out somehow." Anger instantly shoots through me. The flashback to her crying on my chest as she told me how he left her to die plays in my mind. I spent the entire next day digging for his name since she refused to tell me. I should have known she'd have wiped everything clean since she's a computer whiz. I told her I was going to track his ass down. I know she doesn't want me to, but... I've never wanted to hurt someone the way I want to hurt this guy.

"What if she wasn't his?" I ask her softly.

"What do you mean?"

"If she were mine, you guys would be safe. No one would have to know unless you told them. We could say we met when you first got here and hooked up. You said you're about four months along. That means you got pregnant right before you moved here."

She twists in my arms facing me, her eyes sad. "Layton, that's insane."

"I've been spending almost every day with you since you got here. I know you love wearing obscure shirts of bands I've never heard of in my life, I know you would do anything in your power to avoid putting your problems on another person because you'd rather fix everyone else's life than admit for a second that you may need help. I know you are stubborn as hell and that you say you're sorry every day because you don't think you're enough, but honest to God, I have to fight myself to keep my hands off of you all the damn time. I know some piece-of-shit hurt you—almost killed you. And I know that I can help you," I tell her as I wipe the tears from her face. "I won't make you do anything you don't want to do, but I swear on my life, I'd do it if it means you're safe. No strings—we'll know the truth, but to the world she's mine."

"Why?"

"I care about you and I'm trying my best to think of a way to protect you both." I know pretending I'm her dad may not do a damn thing to keep them safe. I'm praying she's right and he really has just let her go, but the voice in the back of my mind keeps whispering to keep her close. The thought of her being in danger makes me crazy and I'm willing to do just about anything to keep her from harm's way.

"I'll think about it," she tells me, twisting away sinking into my hold. I pull her into me, letting my hand rest against her stomach. *I love her... I love them.*

Trish

I let Layton hold me, his hand softly tracing circles across my belly until his breath evens out. I let the tears pour down my face as I ask God why he's given me this beautifully, caring man at the worst possible time. He's everything I could have ever wanted in a man, but I'm so busy trying to pick up the pieces everyone else destroyed. I don't know how to give myself to him.

The sound of Ella in the hall pulls me from his arms, and I quietly sneak through the door quickly drying my eyes with my sleeve.

"Do you need a hand?" I whisper.

"Oh, baby girl. I just was going to get some water. I'm sorry I woke you up."

"It's okay, I was still up. Why don't you go lay down, and I'll bring you in a glass."

"Thank you, sweety. I hate how weak I am. I think I can do more than I actually can."

"It's no problem, I could use a glass too."

I walk her to her bed, helping her get all tucked back in as she grabs my hand.

"Thank you for giving me hope. Please don't tell Layton, but I don't think I'm making it through this one. I'm not as strong as last time. I was so afraid to leave him with no one. I prayed so hard, and then you walked through my door. You were my answer. My sweet boy has a family. He will have you and your beautiful baby girl when I'm gone. He is going to be okay, and you don't know what that means to me," she says, tears streaming down her cheeks. "Promise me, when my sweet granddaughter is here, you'll tell her how much I wanted to meet her.

"I promise," I say, grasping her hand—it's so frail. I wait until I leave the room to collapse in silent sobs. I have no clue how to not break her heart.

Chapter Fifteen

TRISH

The winter air wraps around me as we make our way through the packed stadium down to our seats. I overheard Layton and Tyler talking about wanting to make it to a playoff game. When I saw someone selling two tickets online, I bought them, figuring they could go together. Tyler ended up waking up with the flu, so here I am being shuffled through the dense crowd while Layton looks at everyone like an angry grizzly bear if they get too close to me and my swollen belly.

The last couple months have flown by. Ella let it slip to Claire and Tyler on Thanksgiving that we were having a baby. Layton and I had spent months trying to figure out how in the world we were going to handle telling them both. We'd planned on being honest, but with Ella gushing to them happily about being a mommom, they got thrown into the mess of a lie we'd created.

I kept waiting for Claire to call me out. Instead, she said she figured it out a while ago, but was giving me my space to tell her in my own time. She said she was so excited I was finally getting the life I deserved. I hated how badly that stung, but she was right. I was actually happy for the first time in my life—and none of it was real.

Layton is everything I could ask for, yet I still refuse to make anything official between us. I'm six months along, and the man that's been by my side for every appointment, bad day, and craving while still happily accepting the arm's length I try to keep him.

He doesn't push me for anything more even though I spend every night wrapped in his arms, feeling safer than I've ever felt. One of my favorite things is watching him talk to the baby as she kicks happily at his voice. It's gotten to the point where I have to remind myself that he's not really her dad, and I hate that. He's *everything*. And I still can't move past my past.

"I don't know if this was a good idea," he says for the fifth time. "Please just stay by me so I can protect you guys."

"It's okay, we are safe with you," I say, patting my belly.

"I can't believe you've never watched football," he says as we finally take our seats, and he seems to relax.

"I mean, I've kinda seen it," I say. "My family used to turn it on every Thanksgiving. They came down from upstate New York, so they all loved the *Bills*. My parents used to get so annoyed, they called the players a barbaric overpaid waste of athleticism."

"Okay, tell me what you know, and I will give you a quick rundown of the rest," he says.

"I know nothing."

"Okay, so they will flip a coin to see who gets the ball first. Then the kicker will kick the ball down the field to the receiving team who will have four downs to get it to the next *first* down. If they make it far enough but don't get a touchdown, they can kick a field goal. If they make it to the end zone—that's a touchdown."

I stare at him like he's speaking a foreign language—he might as well be. "So, we want the orange team to run the ball into the big rectangle at the end of the field or kick the ball through the yellow thing. And we don't want the other team to do any of that," he says smirking. "If you have questions during the game, ask me. I like the *Broncos*; they are down there in the blue and orange. The other team is the *Saints*. You wanna pick a team?" he asks, not making fun of me like I thought he would for me not knowing jack about sports.

"How do I know which to pick?"

He shrugs his shoulders. "Growing up, we just looked at all the logos and picked the coolest one."

"Sounds fun to me," I tell him.

He pulls out his phone, typing for a second before handing me it. A bunch of small pictures fill the screen. I look at them all when my eye catches one that has two pirate swords crossed behind a man and it brings me back to a memory of being at my uncles and all the epic sword battles we had with these random plastic swords they found at Walmart. Being the only niece when your dad's brothers were all ten years younger led to some chaotic family functions. My dad called them immature, but I thought they were the best. I feel like the only time I actually got to be a kid was when they went over, once a year.

"That one," I say, pointing at the logo.

He starts cackling alongside me.

"What? Do they suck?" I ask. "I don't even care if they do. That's my team."

"They don't suck, it's just you picked my team's worst enemy out of them all," he says still cracking up. "I love that."

"You *love* it?" I ask arching a brow at him. "Aren't men supposed to be all macho about sports and hate people if they don't like their team?"

"I don't give a shit about that. You like who you like."

I'm not sure why, but that simple remark shoots sparks through me as I stare up at him as he watches the game. I take a moment to just observe him and lean against him and gripping his massive bicep in my palms. Part of me feels like I should be intimidated by his size. Brett was two inches shorter than me and still easily kicked my ass. Layton could ruin me, but there is nothing about him that makes me feel uncomfortable.

The crowd suddenly erupts around me. I look up to see a man crossing the line in front of the big metal yellow thing. He is throwing his arms up and down in excitement as teammates run up and pat him on the back. He takes off jumping up to try and hand the ball to a small girl who has escaped her seat and is now reaching out for the ball next to Layton. She has to be only three or four and can't quite to reach.

"Can I help?" he asks her mom, who is scrambling through the people between them to grab her daughter. She pauses a huge smile taking over her face as she nods her head yes. Layton wastes no time hauling the small child in his enormous grip and holding her up to the ball. The player smiles big at them both and the little girl cradles the ball tightly to her chest as he hands her over the people and back into her mother's waiting arms.

I want to drag him from these stands right now and do unmentionable things. Damn these pregnancy hormones... So much for just being friends.

"Why are you looking at me like that?" he asks when he catches me staring like a weirdo. "You look like you are undressing me with your eyes right now. I feel like a piece of meat," he says with a playful tone to his voice before leaning down and tucking a stand of hair behind my ear. "I'd much rather you undress me with those pretty little hands of yours," he whispers.

A shiver shoots through me that has absolutely nothing to do with the chill in the air. The rest of the game seems to fly by as I jump and cheer with the crowd even though I don't really know what's going on—the enthusiasm is contagious. I catch Layton staring at me a few times, a huge smile across his face.

"That was seriously the most fun I've had in years," I say as we reach his truck in the chaotic parking lot.

"I'm glad you liked it. I was a little worried you'd be bored, but you were the life of the party up there. I think they all liked that you cheered for every single play no matter what team it was," he says, laughing.

He reaches over placing his hand on my belly which is hidden under layers of clothes.

"Baby girl, you hungry in there?" he asks my belly. It growls in response, and he laughs again. "Let's get you both some food before I bring you back home," he says as he pulls out onto the freeway.

The sound of the truck door shutting pulls me from my sleep and I realize I passed out against the window. We are in a shopping center parking lot, and Layton is climbing into his seat, two white paper bags in one hand with an incredible smell pouring from them.

"I got fried chicken; I hope that's okay."

"That sounds so good," I say, sitting up and stretching.

"But before we eat though I may have grabbed you a little something," he says, handing me a third gray bag with a look on his face I've never seen. Like he's worried about how I will react. I reach in grabbing the silky fabric and pull out two Raiders jerseys. One is my size, and the other is itty bitty. "I know you are not a huge football fan, but there is an NFL store that has all the teams. I figured you could have this to remember today. I got nugget one too, to match her mama."

The tears pour down my face before I can stop them, and I am sobbing uncontrollably staring at the matching silver and black jerseys in my hands. I hate that I'm broken. I hate that this man has made it perfectly clear he wants more. I want to give him more, yet that asshole broke me so badly I have no idea how to give even a sliver of myself away. I'm not sure I ever will. This man is giving me everything and hasn't once asked for anything in return, and I hate myself for continuing to take from him. I am holding him back from someone that could give him their heart because I'm selfish and have no idea how to cut him off.

"Shit, I'm sorry, I didn't mean to upset you," he says.

"Layton, this is so freaking nice of you. Like, the nicest thing anyone's ever done for me," I tell him honestly. "I just don't want to be the reason someone doesn't get you. Promise me that. Promise me that if someone else comes along, you will walk away from this. You won't let me hold you back from falling in love."

He pauses, staring silently out the window. I swear I hear him whisper, "I already did." And I know damn well I already did too.

UNCHAIN ME

Chapter Sixteen

LAYTON

The waiting room is packed when we walk in, but it doesn't take long for them to call us back. The minute I hear my mom's name leave the nurse's mouth, my eyes connect with hers, and my stomach drops. I know that look.

The look of sympathy.

I spent the entire day trying to prepare myself for whatever the doctor had to say. Chemo is worse this time. I feel like I'm watching her wither to nothing before my eyes. I keep trying to remind myself that this is hard on the body—it's part of the process. But a piece of me is terrified that this time is different.

The panic only grows as she silently ushers us back into a small white office. I take a seat next to my mom, staring at the desk cluttered with papers in front of us.

"The doctor will be right in for you," the nurse says before closing the door, leaving us alone in the cold room.

"There is a key in my bedroom—top drawer. It opens the safe. All the important documents are in there," she says weakly. I grab her hand; it feels like no more than bones beneath mine and I shove back all of my fears to calm hers.

"Mom, I know where the key is."

"I know, but just make sure if anything happens to me, you go in there first, okay?"

"You are coming home. This is just an appointment."

"Layton, just promise me," she says, locking her eyes on mine with tears already threatening to spill over. "I know you're trying to be optimistic but, baby, I feel it. This time is different. My body is weaker. The cancer is stronger. Maybe I'm wrong and God, I hope I'm wrong, but I don't know how much longer I can fight."

I want to argue with her. Tell her I'm positive she's going to make it through this, but it would be a lie. I'm just as terrified as she is that every word she's saying is true. A soft knock fills the room.

"I promise," I whisper, wrapping my arm around her shoulder as the doctor enters and takes his seat across from us. My mom slowly pulls away, wiping her eyes on the back of her sleeve.

"Ms. Kilier, thank you for coming in. I wish I had better news, but the cancer isn't responding to treatment." The world fades away as I clutch her hand tighter. I want to scream, argue that he's wrong—we're all wrong. She has so much left to live for, she's never had a chance to live. "You're looking at another four to six months. We can try a more aggressive radiation that may give you some more time, but it's not a guarantee."

"I don't want it," she says, her voice the strongest I've heard in months.

"Mom?"

"Layton, I love you so much, but I made up my mind a long time ago. I've given everything I have in me. The treatment is stripping me of what little life I have left. At least this way, I can try to enjoy it."

"You can always call the office at any point, and we can change the plan if you change your mind. For now, I think it would be best to set you up with hospice care."

I bite my cheek until the taste of blood spills in my mouth. I want to demand that he try harder to save her. Beg him to try anything because she's *good*. She's *worth* saving. That's not how this works though, and I don't want to accept that I'm leaving here with a clock counting down the days until I bury my mother.

As we walk back through the waiting room a few eyes shoot up at us. All of them desperately holding on to some amount of hope. Fighting for just another second, not knowing if they will be called in to find out that even their best wasn't enough. My eyes hit a little girl of no more than ten, her parents next to her holding hands, their faces painted in despair. I want to lose it—scream to the sky how unfair this shit is.

Instead, I push forward, the world a blur around me as I make it to my truck and help my mom climb in.

I climb in the driver's seat, but don't start it. I just sit staring forward clenching my jaw.

"Baby, it's going to be okay."

"How?" I ask. "How is it going to be okay, mom? You're dying. There is no way to twist that into some amazing thing, like you normally do."

"Even death has a reason, Layton."

"That's bullshit," I snap. "Tell me the reason I'm going to have to bury you when you're not even fifty, why that little girl is in there with no hair. I'd love to understand what the reason is."

She gives me a soft smile reaching for my hand. "I wish I knew the answers, but that's not my job. I only know that I trust there is a plan. It's what's kept me going all of these years, and it always worked out. Even the times I felt like there was no hope at all, things eventually made sense."

"I'm not strong like you," I tell her, trying not to break down in the parking lot.

"Yes, you are. This is just the biggest test you've faced in your life. When your dad left us, I cried for weeks. I grew from that. Some people grow callused through their pain. Don't let that be you. Let this be proof that life is short, and you need to make the best out of every moment you get. I'm so happy with the life I've lived, and there isn't a single thing I'd change. Not many people can say that."

"I don't know what to do. How do I pull out of this parking lot knowing there is nothing I can do to help you?"

"Life isn't going to stop because I'm gone. You are going to mourn and then you are going to get up and keep going. For yourself, and for the family you're building. I was never supposed to be here forever. That baby and Trish, they're your forever. For now, we make the most of what we have. I'm not dead yet, and I'm starving."

I shove down the guilt of lying about Trish and the baby and look over to her. She's smiling and somehow looks less stressed than when we walked in.

"How are you not freaking out?"

"I told you, I have no regrets about the life I've lived. I know after this, the pain stops and I get peace. I have solace in that. It's like all of the what ifs are done, and now I just know."

I smile at her, trying my best to fake her peace because it seems unfair that she's comforting me when she's the one that should need comforting.

"Benny's?"

"Please, maybe I can get next to Trish on the wall," she laughs.

Mom's exhausted by the time we get home, I carry her to her room and tuck her into bed, kissing her forehead before walking out. I feel like I'm drowning as I walk down the steps towards the bottle of bourbon in the cabinet. I thank God I brought it from my house last week. I'm barely even home anymore because the minute I leave, my mind races with all the what-ifs it could possibly conjure.

I unscrew the lid, taking a huge sip as I sit at the kitchen table, not even bothering to care about the burn that spreads down my throat into my chest. Anger swims through my veins as I take swig after swig, begging the pain to stop. How am I supposed to just sit back and watch her wither away? It tears through me, the pain unlike anything I've ever felt ripping through my chest. The bourbon doesn't do a damn thing to ease it as I drink until the room spins around me.

"You could have had anyone in the world. Why her?" I say to the deafening silence as I lift the bottle to my lips only to realize it's empty.

I stand, grabbing the back of the chair as the world threatens to spin out from under me. Taking my phone, I'm calling *her* before I have time to overthink it.

"I need you," I choke it out as I stumble towards my room, but the second I hit the door, my knees buckle beneath me.

"I'm coming."

Chapter Seventeen

TRISH

My heart hasn't stopped racing since Layton called. I thank God when I see his truck in his mom's driveway. I wasn't even sure where he was and when I called back, it went right to voicemail.

I don't waste time knocking. I just throw the front door open and run up the steps to his room. His door is open, and he is on his knees just past the threshold. I step around and drop to sit in front of him. He looks up at me, tears streaming down his cheeks, and I throw myself into his arms.

"She's dying," he says and I feel the tears break free as I take his face in my hands. "Four to six months, and she's going to be gone."

I just hold him and let him cry. My heart shatters with each shake of his shoulders.

I'm not sure how long we stay like that, but the sky is dark by the time he pulls back.

I know the look in his sad eyes. He's broken, and there's nothing I can do to fix it. I push myself from the ground before reaching for his hand. He takes it, and I help him to his feet and lead him to the bed. He climbs in under the covers and reaches out to me, lifting the blanket in front so I can lay next to him.

"I feel like I should be doing something," he says looking up to me. "It feels wrong. She did everything to give me a great life, and I'm just going to sit back and watch her fade away.

"Well, let's do something then," I say, grabbing a notebook and pen from my bag before running back to climb under the covers. "What are some things she's always wanted to do, but never had a chance?"

"Like a bucket list?" he asks, sitting up and pulling me into his chest.

"Exactly, I know the other day when I was here, she was saying how she always wanted to go to a concert and crowd surf when she was younger. I'm not sure if that's still something she'd like to do, but I'll write it down and we can ask her," I say adding it to the piece of paper.

"She's always wanted to see the ocean," he says. "She used to talk about it all the time when I was a kid.

How she'd love to sit in the sun all day and listen to the waves crash on the beach. We were supposed to go once, but I ended up breaking my leg playing football at the ranch."

"We need to get her there. The beach is the most amazing place ever," I tell him as I jot it down.

"She jokes that she's going to ride a Harley, but I don't think she's joking."

"Your mom is such a secret badass." I laugh, thinking about the sweet woman riding Harleys and crowd surfing.

"I wondered for years what she would be like if she hadn't spent her whole life being a mom."

"Well, let's give her that life."

We sit thinking of things to add. It's not a huge list, but it's something. Some things seem like they are going to be next to impossible to accomplish with her health as unstable as it is, but we add them anyway. We try our best to dig through our memories for anything she's said. Once it's done, we look it over.

Go to a concert and crowd surf.

Go on a date.

Dance in the rain.

Meet her granddaughter.

See the ocean.

Ride a Harley.

"I wish I could think of more," Layton says, collapsing back into the pillow, "She didn't really talk about many of the things she wanted to do. She's always just accepted life for what it was."

"We can ask her when we get up tomorrow if there is anything she'd like to add," I tell him as I trace lazy circles on his chest.

I put the notebook down on the end table and snuggle back into bed. He puts his hand over my stomach dropping his head down too.

"Hey, nugget," he says softly. She kicks his hand, and he looks up to me with a huge smile. "She loves me."

"I know she does," I say smiling as I brush my fingers through his hair. She really does love him. Every single time she hears his voice, she starts moving all around.

"I promise, nugget, I will always be here for you, I love you so much," he says, laying his head against my stomach. "You and your mama."

"We love you, too," I whisper, knowing I am tearing down the last wall I've built. I know giving him this piece of me could destroy me, but I'm tired of holding back. I want all of it. It's only then that I realize he's already asleep.

We walk down the steps into the kitchen, where country music drifts through the walls. Ella is wearing a baby blue bandana covered in kittens wrapped around her head and a smile on her face. She's moving slowly as she flips a pancake on the stove, but she looks more alive than I've seen her in weeks.

"Good morning, guys," she says happily, walking a stack of pancakes to the table. "I cooked."

"Let us help. I got the rest, Mama," Layton says, helping her sit before walking to the fridge to grab out the gallon of orange juice and butter. I walk to the cabinet and grab some plates setting the table.

"I want you both to know something," she says once we are both sitting. "I know the thought of death scares most people, and I won't lie, for a long time it scared me too. I worried I'd be leaving you behind with nothing," she says, grabbing Layton's hand. "Knowing you found someone that makes you happy has given me so much peace. I never feared what comes next. I know where I'm going. I just feared leaving you behind."

"Mama, you never have to worry about me."

"You have been the thing that's given me purpose for the last thirty years. I will always worry about you."

"Mama, Trish and I were talking this morning, and she came up with a plan," he tells her. "We want to help you do your bucket list."

"I don't need to do that," she chuckles. "I'm happy with the life I've lived."

"You've spent your entire life givin' to me. Please, let us do this for you."

She looks at me, a silent question in her eyes.

"Ella, I'd love nothing more than to help you live your dreams," I tell her.

Her eyes instantly well with tears as she looks between us both. "Well, when do we start?"

Chapter Eighteen

LAYTON

I watch Trish and my mom sit in front of the computer giggling as they type something in a dating profile. It feels insane to watch the frail woman in front of me live in a way I haven't seen her live for years.

It's been a couple weeks since she stopped treatment and she's already gotten a huge amount of energy back.

"Write that they have to pick me up on a motorcycle." my mom giggles as Trish quickly types it out.

"I can't even imagine the men you are going to get to click on this," Trish laughs.

"Alright, Layton, do you approve?"

I walk behind them and look at the screen. Her page is titled *I'm dying so please don't get attached*. I cringe but look at her eyes, and she just smiles at me. I'm struggling with her sudden acceptance of leaving, but I'd never let her know that. Her profile picture is one Trish took earlier of her smiling out by her garden. It took them an hour to pick out the perfect bandana.

"I think it's great, mom," I tell her, watching them both light up even more.

"Alright, here we go," Trish says clicking *finished* on the screen.

She jumps from her seat. "I think that was the last thing to do before we head out. Claire just texted me, they're ready."

I let my gaze rake over her; hair tossed in a bun, wearing sweatpants and a hoodie that stretch over her little baby bump in the middle. She looks absolutely nothing like the woman I met five months ago, and I couldn't be happier about that. When I met her, she carried this sadness. Now it is like she found herself.

I walk over to her, wrapping my arm around her shoulder and pulling her into me. I know we have no label except to the world that has this false sense we are dating. It doesn't feel fake to me though. The way we lay in bed every night and share everything, the good, the bad, and the ugly. The way she instantly relaxes when she's in my arms. The way I feel like the weight of everything is just a little less heavy when I'm with her. I want her to be mine. I want to be nugget's dad.

But I'll wait until she's ready. Until she trusts that I would never hurt her the way he did. I will spend the rest of my life proving she's safe with me if that's what it takes.

I walk to the door, grabbing her and my mom's last bag and usher them outside. Wrapping my arm around my mom's waist, I help her to the car. Trish wasted no time at all booking a trip to California. She had the plane tickets purchased as soon as my mom agreed. She wanted to fit as much in as she could in one trip since we have no clue how long she will be strong enough to do it.

Her and my mom looked through all the concerts we could attend. Trish tried to ask her what bands were her favorite, but her response was something to the effect of they are all to lame to crowd surf. They ended up going with some screaming band Trish likes, which has since been blasting through the house at an ungodly volume. I have no idea what is even being said, but my mom smiles happily as she googles the words and sings along with Trish.

"Guys, this is really the craziest thing. I hope you know I would have been happy with anything, but I can't lie and say I'm not excited to see the ocean for the first time."

"Mom, you deserve to get to live, you spent your entire life focused on me."

"I would do it over a million times too," she says looking over at me. "I don't want you to think for one second I have any regrets about how I chose to live my life. If God was to take me right now, I'd go knowing I lived the best life. I owe that to you."

"Mom," I go to argue.

"Don't *mom* me," She chastises. "My number one bucket list item was being a mom. I got to live that dream for thirty years. If that's the only thing I ever got to check off of that list, that is the only one that mattered. Well, aside from being a mommom, that is. I can't wait to meet her, God willing," I hear Trish softly suck in a breath behind me.

Her due date is shortly after my mom will hit the five-month mark. I know there is a chance she may never meet her, and that sucks. She already loves that little girl more than anything in life.

"Don't go getting all sad on me. If I go up before she's here, I'll ask God for a sneak peek. I think he'll give me that. Then I'll just have to come back as a little butterfly every year and visit."

"I love that," Trish says softly, leaning forward to grab her shoulder. "Ella, I love you so much. You are going to be the best mommom this baby could ever ask for, and I'm so grateful for that."

I have so much I want to say, but instead I smile at them both. My words get mixed up in the fact that my mom will be gone soon, and Trish and the baby may leave too. Taking all this fake security my mom believes with her.

I pull out onto the highway. The entire one side of the road is lined with ocean. The GPS leads me a little farther down to a spot to park. White sand lines the roads leading to the beach. The water sparkles under the sun as waves crash on the sand. I've never seen anything like it in my life. It's endless. Like the sky and water keep going until they blur together into one, By the time we left the airport last night and drove to the hotel, it was already dark. Seeing it today, in the light, is amazing.

"This is so much better than I could ever have imagined." My moms voice breaks the silence.

"It really is," I agree with her. "Want to go put your toes in the water?"

"Yes," she says excitedly.

"Ready?" I say looking at Tyler in the mirror. He is also staring out the window like he's seeing a slice of Heaven.

"Let's do this," he says, opening the door. The thick summer heat instantly breaks through the cars air conditioning. I follow him out the driver's side as we all pile out of the car. Trish and Claire grab a couple chairs from the back as Tyler and I get my mom piggyback style on my back. "You feel secure?" he asks her.

"Yup, though a little silly," mom says behind me.

"Piggyback rides are never silly," he tells her. "Layton gives me piggyback rides at work all the time."

"That's something I'd pay to see. Can we add that to the bucket list?"

"I think I'll reserve these for you, mama." I laugh with her before I lock eyes on Trish, whose hair is now down, blowing around her shoulders. The sun beats down on her face as she squints towards me with a huge smile stretched across her mouth as her hand softly rests on top of her belly.

"You ready, darlin'?" I ask her. Her cheeks heat slightly every time I call her that, and I love it.

"So ready, I've missed the ocean so badly."

We walk down the sand and some people look curiously at me, but their looks quickly turn to sad smiles. I try not to let it get to me, but it does. I want to scream at them that she's fine. That I'm not taking my mom on an adventure to live her life simply because she's dying. The regrets of not doing this shit sooner echoes in my mind as my feet hit the water. I softly lower my mom to her feet right as the crash of the waves comes in.

"This is one of the best moments of my entire life," she says quietly, her words choked as she stares out to the horizon.

"You want me to bring you to your chair?" I ask her, looking over to Trish who stands cautiously on the other side of her.

She turns to me, a huge smile on her face as dried lines of tears streak her cheeks. "I want to stand just a bit longer," she says, reaching to grab both of our hands. "Thank you so much for this. Both of you.

"Of course," Trish says smiling at her.

Chapter Nineteen

TRISH

"How long do you think before one of them ends up injured?" Claire says staring towards the boys who have befriended a group of surfers.

"I give them about five more minutes," Ella says. "They sure haven't changed a bit since college, that's for sure."

"I feel like that's generous," I laugh. Less than a second later, Layton busts his ass. Thankfully, he gets up quickly, shooting a thumbs up to us as I'm instantly to my feet, ready to run to save him.

The sun is setting in the horizon casting their silhouettes in front of us. Claire, Ella, and I have been sitting in the sun, watching them for the past few hours. At first, they refused to leave our side. Then Ella brought up Layton's birth story which caused them both to change their minds and run off rather quickly.

"That boy's going to give me a heart attack," I say sitting back down with my hand to my heart.

"I've felt that way since I had him," Ella laughs next to me. "I'd love to say it gets easier, but wait until that baby is here. I don't think I've slept right in thirty years. You'll always worry. That's what happens when you love someone."

Her words hit me. I've known I've loved Layton for months, but for some reason I've felt like if I never told him, it would make it easier. The truth is, if something happened to him right now, it would destroy me. I've built my entire life around him these past few months. He goes to the appointments with me to see the baby. Him kissing my belly and singing her to sleep. Him calling her his nugget. I realize she's more his than she will ever be Brett's—and that terrifies me.

I've already lost everything once and now I'm building a new life that is cracking as I try to put it together. For the first time in weeks, it hits me how much it's going to destroy everything when Ella goes. She's been so happy, embracing the fact that her son has found what she prayed for. What would she think if she knew we've both been lying to her? Trying our damndest to give her the last few months she deserves and unwilling to rip her dreams to shreds, knowing it's the only thing giving her hope.

A panic attack claws at my throat as all the voices I've silenced over the last few months start screaming in my mind. I'm not enough for Layton and his mom, and I damn sure am not enough for this innocent baby girl. The lies are eating at me, and I've embraced them happily but I'm building the same life I did before.

"Trish,'" Layton's voice breaks through my fogged vision. I go to talk, but instead I burst into tears when he kneels down in front of me. "You're okay." His fingers go under my chin to face him. "You gotta breathe for me, darlin'. Whatever is going on in that pretty little head of yours, let it out. I'm here."

I follow his instructions, sucking in a deep breath and focusing my gaze on his dark brown eyes. He slowly rubs my back in soft circles as I breathe in the warm, salty air over and over as the vice around my chest loosens and I feel like I can think clearly again.

He leans back just enough to rest his forehead against mine. "You back with me, darlin'?" he asks softly.

"Yes," I tell him.

"I got her, she's okay. I'll meet you guys over there," he says over my shoulder.

I turn towards them to see Tyler, Claire, and Ella standing right next to me with looks of worry on their faces.

"I'm sorry, guys. I promise, I'm fine. These stupid pregnancy hormones." I laugh patting my belly softly.

"You sure?" Claire asks softly.

"I promise. I just thought about birth and kinda freaked out," I lie adding another one to the pile, but I shove away the guilt.

"Well that's understandable, but you are going to be amazing! We will give you guys a second, and meet you at the car. Tyler and I can help Ella," she says with a smile, accepting my answer. I watch the three of them walk away and turn back to a very unconvinced Layton.

"Can you tell me what actually just happened?"

"I'm so tired of lying to the people I love," I tell him, looking away. "I lie every single day. I have for so long. Coming here, I felt like I was breaking away from it, but I just changed the lies. Before I lied to be someone I wasn't, to fit somewhere I hated. Here, I lie to protect myself."

Understanding flashes across his face. "I shouldn't have asked you to lie about nugget."

"I chose to lie though. At first it was because I didn't want to let your mom down, I was terrified it would destroy her if she knew the truth. Thinking her prayers were answered only to realize that I'm just a fraud. Now I'm struggling to accept the fact that in my mind, you already are her dad. I know it sounds insane, but you do everything. You've been here since day one. The truth feels more like a lie than this." I motion between us. "With you, I know she's safe."

"Darlin', no matter what you choose to do, you and that little girl are mine, I promise you. I want her and I want you. More than I've ever wanted anything in my entire life."

"I don't know what to do," I whisper.

He pulls me into his arms. "Trish, there is no perfect answer in this. It's not like you are lying to benefit yourself. You are lying to protect the people that you love. I wish I could tell you that lying won't come with consequences, but the truth is— no one knows what the future holds. All I know is that I'm all in, either way. We can walk up there right now and tell them all the truth, or I will walk up there and keep being nuggets dad. Either way, I love that little girl as my own.

"I need to be honest," I declare. "I can't spend my entire life faking who I am again. I can't have her grow up and resent me for lying to her."

"Then we tell them the truth,"

"Layton, I lie to you too."

"So, tell me the truth," he says not a hint of anger in his tone.

"I tell you every single day I don't want more than this," I gesture between us. "What if I'm not good enough for you? What if you aren't who you say you are? What if you hurt me? What if you finally realize

I'm not worth all this extra drama? What if she comes, and you realize it's too much?" I ask. "My mind races all day with so many voices still screaming I don't deserve this life. I'm trying to save myself because I don't know if I can handle that pain again. But I know, no matter what, it's going to hurt like hell because I already love you."

"You love me?" he says with a huge smile across his face.

"More than I've ever loved any person ever in my life, aside from this little girl in my belly."

"I would never lay a hand on you, Trish. I swear on my life. If I knew who your ex was, I would have driven hours to beat his ass when you told me. I gave you that gun to use on anyone that tries to hurt you, including my ass. I'd rather die than ever hurt you" he says honestly, leaning down to talk to my belly. "And this little girl? I love her too. Just as much as if she were mine. I'll do everything I can to protect you both, love you, treat you the way you should be treated because you've become a piece of me." The tears stream endlessly down my cheeks. "I will spend my entire life proving that to you. I love you both so much."

"I don't know how to do this. I've spent my entire life trying to mold myself into someone that was good enough to be loved. I'm trying so hard to not become her again. When we tell everyone the truth, I want you to know, no matter what, she is yours," I tell him as he pulls me from the chair, wrapping me in his arms.

"I will be right by your side. I am just as guilty as you." He leans in and kisses me. "Can you tell me you love me one more time?" He says as he leans down, scooping up my chair and walking with me towards the car.

"I love you." I smile at him. "I can't believe I ruined her bucket list night."

Layton stops, twisting me towards him. "You didn't ruin it. I doubt you're the first pregnant woman to cry in the world."

The rev of a motorcycle makes us both look up to see the soft pink flowers of Ella's dress blowing as she has her arms wrapped around a man on a Harley as they speed away while Tyler and Claire stand back, tossing their hands in the air.

We quickly make the rest of the walk to the parking lot.

"You okay?" Claire asks as I reach her side as she wraps me in her arms.

"I'm okay," I say honestly. I will worry about all of the lies once we get home. "Did you guys just put Ella on a random Harley?" I ask, turning to Layton and Tyler. Layton is running his hand through his hair nervously as he paces back and forth.

"She kind of saw it as we hit the parking lot, and the guy was putting his helmet on. She just walked up to him and said, 'Hey can you give me a ride? It's on my bucket list.'"

I can't help but laugh, because the quiet woman I met a few months ago gives no shits right now.

"Well, that's two things off the list," I say grabbing the notebook from my bag scratching through them.

"And what if this random guy doesn't bring her back?" Layton says. But as soon as the words leave his lips, the soft rumble of an engine moves toward us.

The black Harley pulls to a stop in front of us and a huge, bearded man pulls the helmet from his head before quickly reaching down to undo the belt that he's rigged around Ella's waste into his belt loop. He climbs off, helping her off behind him before pulling the helmet from her head. She is cheesing from ear to ear, but when her eyes collide with mine, they go completely serious.

"Oh, sweet girl, are you okay?" she asks, stumbling towards me to wrap me in a hug.

"I'm better than okay," I say holding her tightly against me. "These pregnancy hormones still get to me sometimes. You just rode on a random man's Harley though!"

She twists around to the man who is now talking to Layton—who thankfully looks much more relaxed than he did minutes ago.

"He's taking me out tonight," she says excitedly as she smiles at the man.

He walks towards us with Layton at his side. "I apologize for stealing her like that, she seemed pretty excited about going for a ride and it's not everyday a pretty woman begs to get on the back of my bike," he says and Ellas's cheeks flush next to me. "I'm Henry."

"It's nice to meet you," I say, shaking his outreached hand.

"Well, Ella, I better head out I have to get ready for a date tonight. I think she told me seven-thirty." He laughs walking up to take her hand before leaving a kiss on the top of it.

"She sounds like a lucky lady," Ella jokes, even brighter red than a couple seconds ago.

He walks over to his Harley, smiling at her one last time before putting his helmet on and pulling away.

"Ahhhhh," Ella says chuckling. "He's so hot."

"Mom, do you think this is safe?" Layton asks.

"Honey, I appreciate you worrying about me, but I only have about five months left. I couldn't even walk to the water for goodness' sake. If there was ever a time to risk a date with a random hot biker, it's now."

"Mom, I will worry about you the rest of your life. I don't care how long you got left," he says, wrapping her in a huge hug. "But I also want you to have fun, so I guess I have no choice, do I?"

"She's gonna be fine, man," Tyler says, patting him on the shoulder.

"Yes, and she needs time to get ready. It's already six, so we should get her back to the hotel," Claire tells him.

He looks at me as if asking me what I think.

"I think she's going to have the best date of her life."

"Alright, mama, let's get you back, so you can get ready," he says helping her to the SUV.

Chapter Twenty

LAYTON

The moon shines across the water as I walk down the beach, Trish tucked tightly into my side. Henry came to pick my mom up, and when she walked out in her flower printed dress, he lit up. She whispered to Trish and I that she'd text us she was safe, but not to wait up.

I drug Trish back to the beach after that. I feel like a father that just sent his daughter off to prom with the school bad boy. I'm stuck between this need to protect my mom and realizing protecting her isn't what she needs right now. She seems so light. Like somehow finding out she has an end date has freed her. I can't wrap my head around it.

As I stare out across the ocean, my mind battles with accepting that this is most likely going to be one of the last major memories I have with her. Seeing her today on this beach, covered head to toe as she shivered against even the smallest breeze even in the heat, I realized how quickly she is fading away in front of me. Her dancing around the house with her hair tied up on her head, using the broom as a microphone to belt out some random country song. Every window in the entire house would be open, but she couldn't care less. She'd grab my hand, forcing me to dance with her. I'd pretend to be annoyed until she'd spin me around until we were both in a fit of laughter. I can still see her smile lighting up her whole face as she looked down at me. Looking back, she was always full of life. I've spent so many of these past few years terrified I held her back, but I can't remember a time she seemed unhappy. My mom has always easily found peace in whatever was thrown her way.

Now, I have no choice but to try to find that same acceptance. Life isn't going to stop and wait for me to hop on board. My mom is going to die, and there isn't a thing I can do to change that. I realize I can either enjoy the time I have left with her or let it drag my ass under, drowning me in the pain of it all.

"Do you think it's weird my mom isn't afraid of what's next?" I ask Trish, breaking the silence. "It's almost like knowing she's dying has helped her find peace."

"I think your mom has been fighting for years. That was the only choice she had. For the first time in years, she doesn't have to fight. She's free."

"A selfish part of me wishes she would keep fighting," I say, looking out to the water. "That by some miracle her trying one more time would keep her here."

"I wish that too. I haven't even known her all that long and she's completely changed my life. I had a question about the baby, and I didn't hesitate to call her. I'll never have that with my mom."

"She deserves better than this, and it makes me angry she didn't get that."

"I truly believe your mom loved simply being your mom. That was her dream. I know you feel you held her back from living but, Layton, being a mom was her favorite way of living, and now you are helping her the best way you can to live beyond that."

"I think I'm finally seeing that." I wrap my arms around her pulling her tightly into my chest. I'm not sure how I'd handle this if she hadn't come into my life. "I'm glad she prayed for you."

"Layton," she goes to argue.

"You can say what you want, but I struggled to go day to day, even when I thought she was going to pull through in the end. Finding out I was going to lose her after all of that probably would have sent me over the edge. Having you here these few months has kept my head above water. She wasn't wrong about you being here for a reason. You gave her back her joy. We both needed you."

"I'm just this." She gestures down as if to say something is wrong with her.

"I'm obsessed with every bit of this." I tell her stepping back to look her over in the moonlight. Her t-shirt is pulled tight over her bump, her long legs are uncovered in her shorts, "You are beautiful, your hair has become my favorite color, it's like the leaves of the trees in the fall, I could get lost in your eyes. Your body, God, I could go on and on about your body. If it wasn't so damn inappropriate, I would never stop touching you," I tell her, going to take her back in my arms. She's looking up at me with a smile across her face. "More than all of that though, you're smart as hell, I honest to God think you could do just about anything you put your mind to." I trail my finger above her heart, and I hear her breath catch. I fucking love that sound. "This though. This has to be my favorite part of you, Trish, because I'll be damned if you don't have the biggest heart I've ever seen."

She shoots up on her tiptoes slamming her lips into mine, not a care in the world that there are people walking the beach around us. I obviously couldn't care less either because I match her pace. I'm addicted to every piece of her. I could kiss her for the rest of the night. A soft moan escapes her as my tongue battles hers and a kiss doesn't seem like enough anymore.

"I think I'm ready to go back." She says breaking the kiss. I groan, my mind drifting to thoughts of her underneath me.

The hotel isn't far from the beach.

On the way here, I loved every second of the walk through the warm streets. Walking back with Trish whispering inappropriate shit to me is torture.

We walk through the lobby to the elevators. My prayer is answered when they open empty. The second the doors close, I have her pinned to the wall watching her cheeks heat as a gasp comes from her mouth before I drop my lips to her neck as I push myself against her so she can feel what she does to me.

The ding of the doors opening has me pulling her down the hall to our room. I can't wait to get my hands on every single inch of her.

Chapter Twenty-One

TRISH

The minute we close the door of the hotel room Layton's hands are all over me. Our lips move together like we are both starved. It's nothing like those kisses you see on screen. It's messy and desperate, yet it's still not enough. My fingers slide under his shirt, tugging up on the material as I break apart from him so he can pull it over his head. My hands rake through his hair as he pulls back again, hungry eyes locked on mine as he drops me on the bed.

"Undress for me," he says as his eyes slowly slide down my body.

Suddenly, I am very aware of how different my body looks. My belly that's no longer flat, my thighs that touch, and everything is decorated with stretch marks. I freeze.

"What just happened?"

"Shut off the lights first."

He stares at me for a second, completely confused.

"Why? I can't see you if I shut the lights out."

"That's kinda the point," I say softly.

"No," he says simply.

"Layton."

"Come here right now," he says, his voice stern.

I crawl to the end of the bed before stepping to the floor. He grabs my hand and drags me across the room, stopping in front of the floor-length mirror. I want to curl into myself as I take it all in. The weight that I gained shows everywhere.

"Take off your clothes, Trish," He whispers softly in my ear.

Part of me wants to argue, but I lock eyes with his. They stare at my body in the mirror, his pupils blown with desire. I reach down to the hem of my tank top and pull it over my head reaching back to unclasp my bra, letting it drop to the floor. My breasts sit heavy against my chest. I keep my eyes locked on Layton's as I continue. My thumbs hook into the waist of my shorts as I shimmy them down, taking my granny panties with them. Some things are just not worth living through, and standing here in nothing but granny panties is where I'm drawing the line.

I stand back up, finally looking away from Layton and take myself in for the first time. The body that stares back at me seems like its someone else's, and I instantly regret doing this. I reach up to cover myself, but Layton softly grabs my arms.

"You see these right here?" he says, letting go of my arms to softly cup my breasts. "Every single day I stare at these. I love your tits, Trish. I know soon they will be nugget's, so I'm enjoying them as much as I can until she steals them." His hands drop to my stomach tracing over a couple of the stretch marks marring my skin. "These may be my favorite. Your tiger stripes. You are a badass." His eyes lock on mine again in the mirror as his hands drift over me. "This body is everything, Trish. You're smoking hot. Yes, it's not the same as it was before you got pregnant, but it's just as beautiful. I want to lick every single curve on you. Spend the entire night between these thighs. I know it may take you some time to love your body again, but do not be embarrassed in front of me. This is me telling you, right now, I love every single inch of you. I did before, I do now, and I will after."

He lets go and walks around the front of me, dropping to his knees in front of the mirror. His hands wrapping around the backs of my thighs and his kisses his way down my belly. I watch in the mirror unable to keep my eyes off of the things he is doing to me. His mouth latches over me and a desperate moan comes from my throat. He doesn't stop. He switches from licking to sucking and licking again until I am tumbling over the edge. My fingers pulling at his dark hair as I try not to collapse. My body flush in front of me in full display with the man I am beyond in love with buried between my thighs. He stands up, dragging his pants down his hips, his length springing free. I can't move, all I can do is watch everything he's doing as I clench my thighs tightly together.

He moves back behind me. His hardness pressed against my back as I push into him. I need more—now. He lowers us to the floor. Still facing the mirror that I hate less and less every second. Pushing my front down to the floor he lines up against me before slowly pushing inside.

"Look at yourself, Trish," he says, his voice rough. "Look at how beautiful you are."

Over and over he fills me as he pulls me up against him. My body flush against his as I watch us in the mirror. My tits bounce with every thrust as he fills me. His one hand softly on my throat, the other finding my clit as he begins to rub slow deliberate circles.

Everything about this is too much—I'm overwhelmed by the sparks shooting through my limbs.

UNCHAIN ME

My body is on edge of exploding and the only thing I can do is hold on as the tingling makes its way through my spine. The most beautiful man worships my body as I tighten around him. The world fights to drift away as I come undone. I watch him throw his head back, the moan comes from his lips, and I am gone. I tell him over and over again how in love I am with him, my new mantra, as I let it all disappear.

I'm so glad we kept the lights on.

Chapter Twenty-Two

LAYTON

"I'm convinced you're an angel," Henry says to my mom as he walks her to the SUV. "I never got to say goodbye to my wife. It sounds weird, but it's like I get that chance with you. I got my one more day. You remind me so much of her. When you get up there, tell her I miss her like crazy," he says with a sad smile.

"She will be the first one I run to," she tells him. "I'll have to tell her she picked a good one."

His entire face lights up. He looks gentle even with the leather vest and tattoos. "I appreciate that. I won't forget you, Ella."

He gently closes her door and smiles at us and waves as we pull away. I think I see him reach up and swipe away a tear in the mirror as he fades out in the distance.

I look into the mirror at the three of them. Claire and Trish came out of the bathroom earlier in their matching t-shirts, and dark lines on top of their eyes. My mom in front of them in her wheelchair in the same matching shirt. Instead, they painted her eyes in purple glitter and fake lashes, with a glittery purple bandana to match.

"What a sweet man. In another life, I would have probably fallen in love with him," she says smiling. "I seriously had the best night ever. He took me to dinner on a boat."

"That's amazing, Ella." Trish's eyes meet mine in the rear view. I know its a silent question on how I'm handling all of this.

All of the acceptance I had tried to muster up disappears. Of course she'd be head over heels for a man she can never create a life with. Yet she sits in the back with a smile across her face.

"I see your mind racing up there," she says, and I realize she is also staring me down in the mirror. "I know you don't understand it, but no one is promised tomorrow. Just because I know my time is limited doesn't mean I'm any different than anyone else. I at least can make the best of the time I have. Most people just live every day not realizing the next one is the last. They leave with so many things left undone and unsaid. I won't do that. I'm going to leave knowing I made the very most of every second I had. I'm okay with that. This weekend has been the most amazing time of my life, and as much as I loved the ocean and my time with Henry, I loved making more memories with you most of all."

"I'm working on being understanding like you."

"I know you are. I hope that's something that comes with time." I watch her lay her head on Trish's shoulder. "I love you, honey. I'm going to be just fine." Her words drift off as her eyes close and before too long, she's asleep.

Everyone is silent. I'm sure no one knows what to say. What exactly do you tell a man struggling with accepting he is going to lose his mom? Even without the chemo, its obvious her body is slowly shutting down. I'm just happy she isn't as confused as she was. I know this is no life for her, but I'm a selfish asshole I guess because I still don't want her to go. Even after she tells me it's what she wants. Even knowing she's struggling, I want to beg and plead for more time. More time for me because I need her. Because I'm not ready. Because, damn it, I don't care how old I am, I need my mom. How will I raise this little girl without her guidance? How will I know what to do if she gets sick or cries all night? Who will I call to tell she just took her first steps? I know the reality is she shares her DNA with another man, but screw that. I love her, I want her, and I sure the hell would never hurt her. So as long as Trish let's me, I want her to be mine.

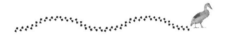

"Alright, how do we go about this?" Tyler yells over the music of the band and crowd.

"I have no idea," I say, looking over at the girls who are having the times of their lives. Trish and my mom both sing at the top of their lungs with Claire laughing and taking pictures on her phone. The sky is full of bright lights shining off the stage as the band starts playing. I still don't know what they are saying, but the energy of the crowd is amazing. The problem is, this venue has a small platform on the beach for wheelchair access, which is nice, but also makes this whole crowd-surfing thing more complicated than we thought it would be.

The song ends and Trish walks up to me, a huge smile on her face, her bright red pin-straight hair hanging down and almost touching the top of her bump. She rarely wears makeup, and she looks damn good without it, but seeing this side of her with her eyes painted dark... It's like I'm seeing another piece of her breaking free. The woman I met months ago was quiet, she over thought every move before doing anything. This woman is the opposite of her, as she laughs loudly throwing herself in my arms.

"I'm going to get some people together to get Ella out there," she says with a huge smile.

"How are you going to do that?"

"I'm gonna climb down and recruit people."

I look down at the belly between us that's making it impossible to get any closer together.

"Darlin', I ain't one to normally tell you you can't do things, but I don't like that plan," I say looking out to the crowd of people in front of us.

"I think I got wrapped up in the nostalgia of all this and had a warp tour flash back."

"You had a what?" I ask, her mouth drops open in shock. "It's okay, how about me and Tyler go recruit people, and you keep your cute ass and my baby girl up here safe?"

"That's a better plan," she says going up on her tiptoes to kiss me. "I freaking love this song."

"Well, go enjoy it. We will be back," I tell her watching her go back to my mom's side. "Ready?" I ask Tyler who is looking into the crowd like he's terrified.

"As ready as I'll ever be," he says, climbing from the side of the platform.

We make our way through the group closest to us. Thankfully, everyone is eager to help and by the time we make it back on the platform, a crowd has formed under us. I look down shooting them a thumbs up before walking over to my mom.

"You ready, mama?" I ask her.

"So ready," she says with a huge smile.

"Well, what are we waiting for?" I tell her as I hoist her up. Tyler is waiting to help me hand her down to the awaiting crowd. I swallow down the slight panic that starts to climb up my throat before I let her go to a group of people I don't know. I shove that shit away. There is no time for worrying anymore.

I let go of her hand fully as I watch her get carried through the crowd. She is cracking up as she moves farther away to the point I can no longer see her face floating gloriously over the crowd. As they move her closer to the stage, I hear the crowd start to chant, but I have no clue what they are saying. But slowly the chant spreads through the crowd.

"Get her on stage, Get her on stage, Get her on stage." Over and over until if feels like the entire beach is chanting. I see the singer throw his hand up to his band and look out to the crowd. His eyes locking on my mom being shuffled over people's heads towards him.

"Well, what's taking you so long? Get her up here!" he shouts into the microphone." The crowd erupts. I don't think half of them even know what the hell they are cheering about, but I'm right there with them as Tyler pats me on the shoulder.

"Holy shit, dude," he yells. "This is amazing."

I see the singer walk to the edge of the stage where someone says something to him.

"We need a chair," the singer says in the mic, and within seconds a chair is run on stage. As the guitar player whips his strap over his head, setting it down and making it to the front of the stage by the singer. They lean down and pull my mom to the stage both getting on either side of her and holding her up as she throws her arms in the air.

"What's your name and how the hell did your adorable self end up crowd surfing up here?"

"My names Ella, I'm trying to live a bit before cancer takes me out."

I cringe, but I'm starting to see a side of my mom I've never seen before. Trish was right— she is a badass.

"Hell yeah, Ella! You want to finish out the concert with us? We have two songs left.

"Hell yeah," she screams into the microphone. Trish is at my side, and I pull her in tight.

"Your mom is a legend."

They walk her over to the chair, setting her up with a mic.

"Ella, this ones for you and all the other badasses out there fighting," the singer yells. The crowd is absolutely feral at this point, but it's nothing compared to the moment my mom sings every word behind him.

"Where in the world did you come from, Ella?" the singer says on a laugh mid-song. She just smiles, looking like she's on top of the world.

Chapter Twenty-Three

TRISH

"Look what Tyler just sent me," Claire says, showing her phone to Ella. "You're famous."

"I am not." She laughs. "I still can't believe they let me sing. Now the world will remember me for how terrible my voice is."

"The world will remember you for being a badass that got to sing with *Sleep Inside*," I tell her.

"That was pretty badass, wasn't it?" Ella asks, pointing to a pink car seat stroller set next to us. "What about this one?"

"Oh my gosh, Trish, it's perfect. Look how cute!"

I look over to the car seat, stroller combo. It's all baby pink with cute frills on it. I love it and as I walk up, I see the tag has a tiny yellow butterfly on it. I wasn't sure if I was going to have a theme for her but the more we shop, the more the most adorable butterfly-print things keep popping up. Every time I see something new, I just think about what Ella said that day about coming back as a butterfly. I decided she was going to be surrounded by them.

"That's perfect," I say adding it to the list so it can be delivered to the house.

I know Ella will try to pay for everything today, but I refuse to let her. Not while knowing I'm still hiding the truth. Layton insists she won't love her any less, and in my heart I believe him, but it still feels wrong. We had planned to sit her down as soon as we got back from our trip, but it took a lot out of her. A week has gone by since we got back and she's just gotten worse.

Hospice came yesterday and confirmed our fears. They said they think she has another two weeks. Now there is this constant battle of wanting to beg her to rest and not holding her back from the things she wants to do. It seems like the time that was already so small is going quicker than we could have ever imagined. So, when she asked to go shopping to get all of the last-minute things today, I couldn't say no.

I know she knows there is a very good chance she will never hold this baby. Even though everything in me wants to tell her, the thought of her hating me is making it next to impossible.

"The only thing left is the monitor, and you should be all set for her to come," Ella says happily.

"I can't believe I'm going to be an aunty in just over a month!" Claire says as she pulls a tiny blue dress from a hook. "Oh, she needs this one."

"She's never going to be able to wear all these clothes." I laugh as she tosses it in the pile of five other dresses she already insisted she needs on this trip alone.

"Aunty Claire will change her outfits during the day, like the little diva she is," Claire says.

I look at her and Ella now looking through the clothes as well, and I can't help the smile that comes across my face. Having these two is the most amazing blessing I could ask for. I finally called my parents last week to let them know. I know how horrible that is, but I've dreaded it. They said, and I quote, "What a waste of your intelligence. Don't expect any support from us. You can figure out your mistakes by yourself." The anger I felt at them calling her a mistake was unmatched. Sure, her father isn't my first choice, but this little girl will never be a mistake. I re-blocked their number as soon as I hung up the phone.

"I think we're ready," Ella tells me, now holding a dress of her own. "Can you save this one for her first birthday? You don't have to put it on her for her birthday, but it can be my gift to her?" she asks looking at the tiny yellow dress with purple butterflies covering it.

"Of course, I will."

"Thank you," she says. "I was hoping I'd get to meet her. I don't have another month in me." For the first time, I see the sadness in her eyes as she reaches softly touching my belly. "Mommom loves you."

As soon as Claire starts pushing her towards the cashier, I text Layton.

> We are telling your mom tonight.

> Sounds good to me. Is everything okay?

> Should have done it sooner. I can't lie to her anymore.

> I know. We will tonight as soon as I get home. Helping Tyler with the barn roof. Got a hole from last nights storm. I'll be home around six. I love you.

> Be safe. I love you too.

I catch up to Claire and unload the entire cart on the belt.

"This baby has more stuff than most adults," I say looking at the insane number of things lining the belt. Right now, we have no idea where we are even staying. I have all my stuff at Layton's mom's currently, even though Layton has an entire house. With his mom being sick, it is impossible to go there. He said he doesn't want to take her from her house since it's where she's most comfortable, which is completely understandable.

Claire has basically moved into Tyler's house, with the exception of Michael's stuff. I know she's only keeping it there because she doesn't know what I'm doing. I don't even know what I'm doing. Neither of us are ever at the house anymore. Layton keeps telling me to move my stuff to his house, since at this point it's just a waste of money. I just want to be honest with Ella before I cut the final ties, just in case it blows up in my face.

"I have to run to the house and grab a couple things before I head back to your house, Ella. Is that okay?"

"If not, I can drop her off and sit with her until you get back," Claire offers. "I drive right by it on my way to the ranch."

"I think I will just head home then you don't have to rush. I could use a nap," she says.

"Okay, if you're sure?" I ask Claire.

"It's no problem at all."

"Thank you. I'll only be, like, ten minutes."

We walk to the cars and help Ella in Claire's car before we load Ellas's car with all of the stuff.

"Alright, that's the last bag," I say, tossing it in the back. I wrap Claire in a hug. "Thank you for everything."

"Of course, you are my best friend. I love you. Now, go get your stuff and get your cute pregnant butt home."

"Okay," I laugh. "I'll see you soon."

I climb into the driver's seat and head to the house. I turn the music up and singing at the top of my lungs to a song by *Sleep Inside.* Not caring if anyone sees. I am so ready to be free, and after tonight there will be no more lies. I will let it all out, once and for all.

I pull in the driveway, and park, shutting off the car and silence once again fills the air. The house feels so empty now. I walk into my room grabbing a few more oversized t-shirts since I'm quickly outgrowing everything that fits, before walking through the house making sure there is nothing else I need.

As I'm walking to the front door, I realize it's already almost six. I grab my phone, hitting Layton's name as I swing open the door. In front of me stands Brett.

I've never seen him seem so out of control. His eyes are wild, hair unbrushed sticking up across his head.

He looks like the monster he actually is. It's terrifying. He looks down at my stomach with disgust as he tosses a pile of unopened mail at my feet.

"Miss me?"

"Brett, why are you here?" I say as he steps forward, forcing me further into the house.

"Your mom got tired of waiting for you to figure out how to get your mail fixed, so she sent me to deliver it. She told me you called and told them you were knocked up by some red neck. She's worried about you, Trish. She wanted me to talk some sense into you. Convince you to come back with me." I stand frozen, pinned between him and the wall.

"That's not going to happen," I tell him, trying to hold my voice steady, hoping he can't tell how much I'm praying Layton pulls up and saves me.

"You never said goodbye. I woke up, and you had packed all your shit and left. How do you think that made me look? I had to lie to my dad about what happened. Then he brought up the party and said he changed his mind about handing over the company to me because he didn't like how I'd been handling myself." He laughs manically. "Said it had been brought to his attention, I didn't treat you well. The thing is, it was you that constantly made me look bad. You couldn't just show up, look nice, and shut your mouth. Then you went and ran your mouth to him after you left." He looks me up and down, repulsed. "It hasn't even been a year, and look at you."

I wait for the shame to hit me, but it doesn't. I realize I couldn't care less what he thinks of me.

"Then leave," I say, standing up straighter, scooting to the side, keeping my eyes on Brett as I try to get away from the wall. "I never talked to your dad. Anything he heard was from other people who saw who you really were before I even saw it myself."

"You ruined my life. You think I'm just going to let that go? Let you come here and live happily ever after with some ranch hand and your bastard child? Babe, I have nothing to lose," he says, stepping forward.

Without thinking, I reach into the holster Layton bought me, pulling out the pistol and aiming it at him. He freezes, putting his hands up before stepping back.

"I think you thought you were going to come here and the Trish that left was still going to exist and maybe feel bad for you. She'd do anything in her power to make you happy. Sorry to disappoint you, Brett, but that girl is gone. The truth is, I don't feel bad you lost the company. You almost killed me!" I say, keeping the gun aimed at him as I take the final step away from the wall. My entire body is trembling, but this time I can't be weak. I need to protect my child and I *will* do everything in my power to do that.

"What are you going to do, you dumb bitch? Shoot me? I wish you had died that night, then none of this would have happened. Everyone would have pitied me. I'd be running everything. That's what was supposed to happen. I refuse to go back to nothing. You're either coming back with me, so you can tell my dad this whole thing was a big misunderstanding—hell, I'll even pretend the fucking thing is mine and show my dad I'm capable of taking over—or one of us isn't leaving this house alive." He laughs, moving his arms out convinced I won't do anything.

"I've spent my entire life trying to make everyone else happy, Brett. I'm tired of it. I realized, thanks to that 'ranch hand', I didn't need anyone to fix me. I just had to get the courage to unchain myself from your unrealistic expectations. I don't need you. I never needed you. You just manipulated me into thinking I did. I will never let that happen again."

"Well then, please, pull the damn trigger, Trish. Kill me because if you don't, I won't hesitate to finish the job this time," he says,

The reality of what pulling the trigger really means hits me. The monster in front of me morphs into the man I once loved. I take off running towards my room, realizing I may have just cost my daughter and I our lives, and I hate myself for that.

He slams into me from behind. My body smashing hard into the ground with his weight on my back. Pain bursts through the side of my head as his fist connects. Stars bursting behind my vision, the gun pinned between me and the floor digging painfully into my stomach.

"You stupid fucking bitch," he screams, his fist landing again, this time on the back of my head. "You'll always need me. You're nothing without me."

I know my only chance is pretending he's won. I go limp beneath him, praying it's enough to make him let up. It seems to work. He pauses, climbing to his feet before kicking me hard in my ribs. It takes everything in me not to scream out in pain at the impact, but I swallow it down.

The sound of the front door opening breaks the silence.

"Trish," Layton's voice fills the air, my eyes burst open to see the gun in Brett's hands pointed right at me. The second Layton walks into the hall, he swings the gun towards Layton.

"No!" I scream, ripping the gun out from under me, squeezing the trigger. The sound of a gunshot fills the air.

Chapter Twenty-Four

LAYTON

"Hey, darlin', we just wrapped up. I'll be home soon," I say pinning the phone between my ear and shoulder as I help Tyler load the last of the wood into the truck bed. The line is silent. "Trish?"

"Brett, why are you here?"

The wood falls from my hand crashing to the ground as the world spins around me. *No.*

"We gotta go," I yell as the call drops. "We gotta fucking go." I'm frantic as I jump into the passenger seat. Tyler jumps in the driver seat taking off through the ranch.

"Where am I going?" he says.

"I don't know. Trish is in trouble."

I realize I have no clue where she is. They were shopping, but that was hours ago.

I quickly call my mom's phone.

"Hey, baby," she says happily.

"Where's Trish?"

"She had to run to the house to grab a couple things. Is everything okay?"

"She's at her house," I tell Tyler as we reach the road. He still has no clue what's going on but speeds out on the road toward the house without question.

"I have to go, mom. I'll call you back," I say as she asks again if everything's okay, but I end the call.

What the hell is going on?" Tyler asks, not even bothering to fully stop as he flies through a stop sign.

"He found her," I say as I dial 9-1-1.

"Who?" Tyler ask.

"Nugget's dad," I say in a panic.

He looks over to me, questions written all over his face, but he doesn't say anything.

I hear the sirens in the distance as we pull up to the house. I don't wait for Tyler to fully stop before I jump from the truck, pulling out my gun and running to the house. Tyler is right behind me. My legs shake with every step I take—not knowing what I'm about to walk into.

"Trish?" I shout as I make it to the hallway and my eyes lock on her, crumbled in a ball on the ground as he kicks her in the ribs. She doesn't move. My heart drops, begging her to do something to let me know she's still with me. He's over top of her with a gun pointed at her head before turning it towards me. Everything freezes as I raise my gun towards him. He's quicker. A gunshot fills the air as I pull the trigger.

My eyes locked on Trish. The bang is deafening as Brett collapses on the ground, vacant eyes staring ahead. I thank God his aim is shit as I rush to Trish's side.

She has a bruise forming on the side of her face already, and she winces when she moves.

"He shot you," she screams, wincing as she throws herself at me.

"He missed," I tell her. "Darlin', I'm right here. I'm okay, I promise. I need to know you're okay."

"I didn't want to kill him, but he gave me no choice," she cries. "He gave me no choice."

"I shot too, Trish. He had a gun, he was hurting you," I say trying to look her over as she winces in pain grabbing her stomach. "You gotta tell me what happened, so I know how you're hurt."

"He hit me from behind. I hit hard. Then he kept punching me. I've been having contractions ever since, I shouldn't have hesitated. I was supposed to protect her. She has to be okay," she rambles as panic starts to set in. She collapses into my chest, crying hard. "I was so scared."

"It's going to be okay," I reassure her, ignoring my heart pounding in my ears as I watch the ambulance and police whip into the driveway.

"I'll bring them to you guys," Tyler says running out the front door as someone shouts for him to put his hands up.

"What if we get in trouble?" she asks, wincing through a contraction. This time digging her nails into my hand through it. This one was longer then the last and I am freaking out on the inside.

I pull her into me. "You have nothing to be afraid of, he came into your house. He hurt you. We did what we had to do to protect you both, now he can never hurt you again. He can never hurt nugget."

She bends over, grabbing her stomach as another contraction tears through her. They are too close together. *Where the hell is Tyler?* Fear races through me at the fact that it's too early for her to be in labor. I can't add any more stress to her right now. I can freak out later, on my own time. Now, she needs me.

"Layton, she can't come yet." She cries as Tyler finally comes through the door. He looks as frantic as I feel, with an EMT on his heels.

The EMT looks around, taking in the scene before kneeling down by Trish. "Miss, is any of this blood from you that you're aware of?" he asks her.

"I don't think so. I'm having contractions, though. I'm only thirty-four weeks."

"Okay, we are going to get you taken care of. Can you tell me what happened?" he asks as he looks her over.

I listen to her describe him cornering her as she opened the door, him chasing her down the hall and punching and kicking her as I watch another EMT cover the body with a white sheet. I've never been so angry I couldn't hurt someone as I am now. He was going to take them from me. He was so selfish he would have rather she die than let her live her life in peace.

My happiness. My world. He wanted to steal it all. Knowing you love someone so much that at any point can be ripped away from you is the most terrifying thing I've ever had to accept. Trish and Nugget are no different than my mom. They aren't invincible. At any point, their lives can end and there isn't a damn thing I can do to stop it.

It's truly terrifying to love someone so much that you know their life ending would tear you apart. What's more terrifying is the thought of never truly knowing love at all. I know my mom is going to die, but I wouldn't go back and trade all of the memories with her to escape the pain of her loss. Same goes for Trish and Nugget. I know I'm not promised forever, but attempting to live a life without them would be no life at all.

I watch them load Trish onto the stretcher, her hand still tightly grasped in my own as I pet her hair out of her face, telling her over and over everything will be okay even though I don't know anymore than she does .

"You have to meet us down there, *Lady of Saints*." The driver tells me, patting me on the shoulder. "We will take great care of her."

"I love you, I'll meet you there," I tell her, letting my hand fall from hers as they push the doors closed. The sirens tear through the air as they pull away.

"Fuck," I yell, dropping to my knees.

I hear the officer in front of me asking a million questions. The answers leaving my mouth but none of it feels real. I shouldn't still be here. I should be with her.

"Alright man, I got it all. If they need anything else, they can meet you down there." The officer says, breaking my trance as he walks away.

"I know this is a lot, but you need to get up," Tyler says, reaching down for my hand, "Nugget's going to be okay, but Trish is going to get there and be alone. She needs you there."

"What if she's not?" I ask him, reaching for his hand.

"Then she will need you by her side even more."

I know he's right. I need to be there. I let him take my hand and me from the ground. I get my shit together as I run to the passenger side of the truck.

He drives like he did when we were teenagers—flying through the dirt roads of the ranch, mud flying over the truck and taking turns on two wheels with his flashers on.

"I'm beating that ambulance," he says, turning another corner. My mom is right, meeting Tyler saved my ass. And as he risks my life driving like a maniac to get to my girl, I know I could never find a better friend than him.

He slows down, pulling into the parking lot driving right up to the entrance. "Thanks, Tyler," I yell jumping from the truck.

"I'm grabbing Claire. We will be right back," he says out the window as he pulls away.

I waste no time running inside and going to the front desk. Thankfully, I recognize the woman as one of my mom's friend's, Marie, who she used to work with.

"Layton?" she asks, taking in my frantic state.

"Trish Beckett," I say.

She types in her name on the computer.

"She is just being brought in now. They are taking her right to labor and delivery. Through these doors, all the way down the hall to the left, and you'll see the sign. She's headed to room 145."

"Thank you, Marie," I say, taking off down the hallway without another word.

Chapter Twenty-Five

TRISH

Preterm labor after killing my abusive ex was not in my birth plan. I know that's something I will have to face sooner or later. Right now, though, I stare at the screen in front of me as the ultrasound tech squeezes warm gel onto my stomach and moves the wand across it. Layton squeezes my hand tighter. The silence of the room is unnerving after the chaos we just went through.

The soft whooshing of her heartbeat fills the room as she finally takes shape on the screen. I focus on the noise filling the air as the tech continues her scan, and almost all of my anxiety dissipates.

"Everything looks great," she says as she wipes off my belly, shooting relief through me. "The doctor is going to head back in shortly and talk to you both."

My body aches, my mind is shaken, but my heart, thank God, isn't shattered like I feared it might be. I hear Layton release a breath next to me as his hand loosens.

"She's okay," he says. "She's okay." I know he is reassuring himself because even though he sat here telling me over and over it was all going to be okay, I could see the panic behind his eyes.

He doesn't wait for the tech to leave before he wraps his arms around me the best he can across the hospital bed, to hold me. A contraction hits me, and I try my best to breathe through it, but nothing truly prepares you for the pain. By the time it passes, there is a doctor in the room.

"Ms. Beckett, I'm Dr. Palo, I will be your physician tonight. I understand you sustained some trauma prior to these contractions. I just reviewed your scans, and the baby seems to be doing great," he says, coming to sit in the chair at my bedside. "Situations like these ones can be really tricky. Normally, we would give you something to try and slow labor, but she has had a few decelerations in her heart rate since you've been here. There is nothing to worry about now, but I feel it would be best for you and the baby to let you continue to labor."

"Is she going to be okay coming this early?" Layton asks as another contraction hits me. Thankfully, the doctor waits until it passes. "Thirty-four weekers generally do really well, but be prepared for her to potentially need some time in the NICU. As soon as she's out, they will check her weight and breathing to see how she's doing and we'll evaluate our options from there. There's no real way to know until she's here, but our NICU team is fantastic. If she does have to spend some time there, I promise she'll be in great hands."

"Thank you," I tell him, trying my best not to worry about the what-ifs.

"If you have any other questions, don't hesitate to press the call button," he says standing to leave, "Layton, congratulations, son," he says before walking out of the room.

"How do you know so many of these people?"

"My mom worked here for years before she got sick."

"She worked at the hospital? I thought she worked at a school?" I laugh realizing I forgot cafeterias existed outside of a school setting.

"Nope, she worked here. Everyone loved her. I think she was the most popular person at every work party," he says smiling.

I smile before doubling over. "Frick," I say letting the pain subside as Layton rubs soft circles on my back.

There is a soft knock, and someone walks in.

"Trish, my name is Dr. Ravin. I'm a psychiatrist. Dr. Palo called me to see if I could come talk to you, to see how you are feeling."

I freeze, I had made up in my mind I was going to pretend everything that happened today hadn't happened. With the intense pain every few minutes, it's been pretty manageable until this moment.

"You don't have to talk if you are not ready. You went through quite a lot today. I just want you to know I'm here for you for the rest of your stay. If I'm not here, one of my colleagues will be."

"Honestly, I'm not sure I've even had a chance to let it all sink in yet. On one hand, I feel like I should feel guilty. I'm sure there will be a time when the guilt will hit that I took someone's life."

She walks over sitting alongside me. "It may or it may not, you guys did what you had to do to protect yourself and your baby. There is no perfect way to handle the ramifications of that."

I swallow, trying to decide if I'm a monster for not mourning Brett at this moment. "Another part of me though, has so much anger that he gave us no choice. That he put me in a situation where he'd rather die than just let me finally be happy. He hurt me and wanted to hurt my baby. Now she has to come before she's ready because he was so selfish. I have so much hatred towards him. I'm not sure I'm even ready to figure out any of it," I say a contraction breaking my rant.

"Take your time," she says, holding my hand until the contraction passes. "I'm sorry to bother you while you're in labor. When this baby comes, the first thing you're going to do is shove yourself to the side. You both went through something traumatic today. All of your feelings are valid, and they will continue to change every day. I would highly recommend both of you seeing a therapist once you leave here. As hard as it may be to put yourselves first, this is important."

"I promise, we will," I say looking over at Layton.

"Good. Layton, I'm holding you to it. I'm going to let you guys have a little more time to yourselves before you bring that baby into this world," she says before leaving the room.

"Do you think we did the right thing?" I ask him.

"I think if we didn't, there is a good chance we wouldn't be here right now."

"I don't know how to erase his face from my mind. There was a time I loved him, and now I have to live the rest of my life knowing I took his life. I hate that he has somehow found a way to haunt me after this. The only thing that keeps fighting back is I can live with him being dead. I couldn't have lived if he hurt Ella."

"Ella?" he asks, and I realized what I've said.
"I planned to ask you if it was okay first."
"Of course, it's okay. It's perfect."

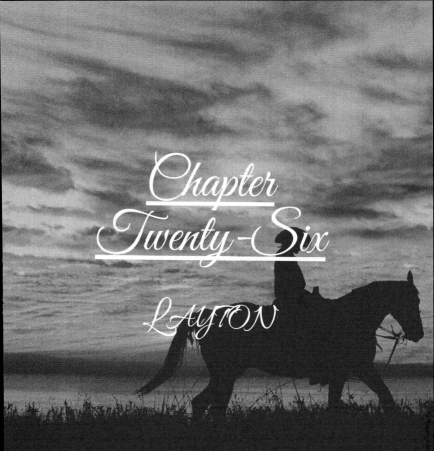

Chapter Twenty-Six
LAYTON

I feel completely worthless as I watch Trish shake in pain, trying her best to bring baby Ella into this world. I let her squeeze my hand until I'm pretty sure it's broken, and I try my best to tell her how much of a badass she is but there are no words to describe her in this moment.

I've been here with no more than stupid encouraging words and ice chips for the last ten hours while she's been in the most pain I think I've ever seen a person experience. None of the books I read prepared me for what it's like to watch a woman go through labor and birth. It's completely unfiltered and raw. It's messy and chaotic. It's truly incredible that a person is capable of something so intense, and it happens like it's just another normal day.

I hold her hand tighter, and she pushes through another contraction. I can tell she's losing her strength with each wave. Her hair is plastered to her forehead, and no one has offered her a washcloth to cool her down. In all the movies they have a washcloth. I want to demand someone give me something to cool her down, but I also don't want to cause any more stress than I need to, so I pull my sleeve over my hand and wipe the sweat off of her face.

"Give me one more big push and you will have your little girl in your arms," the doctor says.

Trish seems to get a second wind and gives it everything she's got. Her entire body trembles and she fights to bring our little girl into the world.

"You got this, darlin'," I tell her. "You are so strong, you are amazing, You're about to be a mama—" and in what seems like a blur, the pain etched into her face turns into relief and a tiny little girl is set onto her chest, *screaming*.

This, right here, is the absolute best moment of my life. Right here, right now, seeing the tiniest human I've ever laid eyes on and realizing I love her more than anything in this world. She instantly calms once she's skin to skin, against Trish's chest.

"You did it, Trish, she's perfect," I whisper, looking at them both.

I don't even realize there are tears pouring down my cheeks until Trish reaches up, swiping one away.

"Dad, you want to cut the cord?" I look at Trish. She smiles and nods her head.

"She's yours, Layton. She's never been anything less than yours."

I smile—she is mine, and I will do everything in my power to give her the best damn life I can.

I look over at Trish with baby Ella tucked tightly against her chest. The nurses in the NICU have been amazing with us over the last couple days. We've both been so grateful for them helping us deal with the fear of having her away from us. Having to sit back and watch someone so tiny covered in so many wires is scary, but they are pros.

I look up to see Claire pushing my mom into the room.

"You made it!"

"I wouldn't miss this for the world."

"I'm going to let you guys get some mommom time, I will be back later to see her," Claire says backing out of the room and blowing Trish a kiss.

"Ella, I need to be honest with you about something that I should have told you a long time ago."

"You can tell me anything, baby girl."

"When I came here, I was trying to get out of an unsafe relationship. I met you guys before I knew that I was pregnant. When I found out, you thought it was Layton's baby. Instead of being honest, we made up a plan to lie to you. Part of me didn't want to hurt you, but another part of me just liked the lie so much better than the truth. After that, I was so afraid you wouldn't feel the same about us. I didn't know how to tell you the truth."

"Her dad, he's the man that hurt you guys?" my mom asks softly.

"Yes, that was him."

"Well, I'm glad you killed him, then," my mom says, causing Trish's jaw to drop. "Baby girl, the day you walked into my life, I knew I loved you. These past few months, you've given me back my courage to live life. You brought my joy back, and you loved me even on my worst days. I don't care who you made that little girl with. I care about *you*. I care that you love my son and you both are safe."

Trish wipes the tears that fall down her cheeks.

"You wanna hold your granddaughter, mama?" I ask her.

"More than anything in the world," she says as I climb up, walking over to Trish.

"You okay?" I whisper, leaning over to kiss her on the head.

"Better than okay," she says, handing me our sweet baby.

I kiss her gently on her head too, as I walk her to my mom. Setting her down in her arms, my mom instantly bursts into tears looking down at her.

"Oh, Trish, she's perfect," she says, looking across the room to Trish who is crying just as hard. "I've been lying to you guys all these weeks. I said I was going to leave here without feeling like I missed out on anything, but the truth is, knowing I was never going to meet this sweet girl has been killing me. I wanted this more than I've wanted anything. Now I've really lived every single dream."

"Ella, there is no way I can ever thank you for being a part of my life these past months. I can never tell you how much knowing you has changed me. I spent my entire life without a mom that loved me. Then I met you and I learned exactly the mom I want to be. I love you so much," Trish tells her through her tears. "I decided on Nugget's name months ago, but it didn't feel right until I was honest with you. We named her Ella—after you, so she always has a piece of you with her. I couldn't think of a better person for her to be named after."

"Oh, my sweet girl," she says, sobbing as she holds baby Ella tighter into her chest. "Thank you so much. God couldn't have sent me a better person than you."

I smile sadly at the scene in front of me, accepting that I'm looking at the exact definition of my past meeting my future.

Chapter Twenty-Seven

TRISH

"You want to rock her?" I ask Ella.

"Please, this is my favorite part of the day," she says reaching out with grabby hands. I wrap my little girl tightly in a blanket, her bright red hair sticking up crazily on top of her head. Ella doesn't have much strength left, and I swear she saves every ounce of her energy to get her mommom snuggles in. Layton somehow found a place to make bandanas with matching baby blankets. Today's theme is yellow lemons, and I can't help but smile at how adorable they look together as Ella hums her a song while she rocks back and forth.

"I can't believe she's a month old tomorrow," I say smiling over at them. "It's crazy to think that I probably wouldn't have ever met her." Hospice was here a couple hours ago, and they said she only has a couple days left. I hate knowing her body is failing her. "I'm so glad I got all of this time with her. I never thought I'd get to see her face, and somehow, I've had an entire month being her mommom. I couldn't have asked for more."

"How did you do it? I fear constantly. I just hope we do good enough. It's so hard to know what she needs. Last night, she cried for an hour straight and nothing helped," I say thinking of me and Layton frantically trying everything we can think of to help calm her down. "Finally, she puked down the front of him and fell right to sleep."

"There is no book that shows you how to parent perfectly." She laughs seeming to reminice her own parenting woes. "Give yourselves grace. You guys are babies to this as well. Learn together and try not to be too hard on yourselves. Love her with everything in you, and the rest will fall into place. Loving your children doesn't mean you won't make mistakes. It means you'll love them enough to never stop trying to be better."

"Thank you, you always know how to make me feel better about everything. I feel like this is how it was supposed to be to have a mom."

"Well, to me you are my daughter in my heart forever," she says smiling. "I knew the day you walked up to me that I loved you. You have a fire inside of you, Trish. That's something to be proud of and I hope you never put it out for anyone ever again."

"Now that I know what it's like to live again, I'm never going back."

"Have the nightmares gotten any better?" she asks, concerned.

"Therapy is helping. I'm glad Layton made me go. I was so sure I'd know if it all got to be too much, but I feel like I got in over my head before I realized it was an issue. I feel bad I missed it."

"Sweety, you did the best you could. Balancing everything you went through before you came here, that night and having a baby is a lot. Never feel guilty about that. Layton understands."

"I know he does. He's the most patient man I've ever met."

"Trish, I need you to promise me something."

"Anything," I tell her.

"Don't drown yourselves in the loss of me. You've both been through so much this last year. I'm going to leave this earth and there is nothing anyone can do to stop that and I know you two are going to hurt.

You know I've found my peace. I've lived my life and enjoyed every second of it and while there are so many things I'm going to miss. I wish I didn't have to but I need you to know I'm ready to go. You two have so much life ahead of you. I don't want you to miss out on a second of your future because my death held you back."

"I promise." I say, even though it seems damn near impossible.

"Thank you," she says looking down in her arms at a now sleeping baby. "Look at that, this chair works every time."

"Do we have an umbrella?" Layton's asks bursting through the back door.

"Front closet?" I tell him as he runs over, throwing open the door, grabbing out an umbrella, and tossing it in my hands walking up to his mom.

"Can I take her, mama?" he asks.

"Of course, baby,"

"Why do I have an umbrella?" I ask him looking out the window at the perfectly sunny sky as he loads the baby into her car seat, somehow not waking her up.

"You'll see. The diaper bag is in the truck, I'm going to grab my mom, then I'll come get my baby girl.""Ready, mama? We're going to the ranch. I want to show you something," he says, scooping his mom in his arms before walking out the front door. I have no clue what Layton has planned, but I take my umbrella, waiting as he comes and grabs the little pink car seat before I follow him out to the truck.

He looks over, smiling at me, before pulling out on the road. I look in the rearview mirror at his mom as she hums a song while smiling down at our baby girl. It doesn't take long before we are pulling into the ranch. Layton drives past the driveway, all the way to the back of the barn where we watched the sunset months ago. I look around, still completely confused when music starts playing from the barn. The door is wide open, and Luke is sitting in the corner with a laptop in front of him. I see a bunch of the ranch hands sprinting around turning on hoses that spray into the air, raining down into the center of the barn and turning the dirt to mud.

There hasn't been a speck of rain for weeks, and I realize that's the only unchecked bucket list item. *Dancing in the rain.* I look at him and take in everything as I fall even more in love with him. He unclips Ella, handing her to me before opening and passing me the umbrella.

"I'm not letting her go without finishing that list," he tells me, leaning down to kiss me before he walks to the back seat, opening the door and carrying his mom out.

I hit the barn feeling the warmth from the heater as I follow him inside.

"Let's go dance in the rain, mama," he says as he hits the center, his mom's laugh filling the rooms as the water crashes over them.

Soon, everyone is drenched and the laughter is so loud, it almost drowns out the music. We dance until the sun has sunk low in the sky. Baby Ella is tight against my chest, my tears swallowed by the rain, as I watch the man I love say goodbye to the woman that changed our lives.

The End

Epilogue

TRISH

I walk into the kitchen where Layton holds Ella, dressed in her little purple butterfly dress from her mommom. Her bright red hair sticks straight up into the air. He's looking at her like she's hung the stars as he dances with her to some country song he has blasting on the radio and her tiny giggles fill the air.

"Come on, darlin'," he says, reaching out to me. I reach out my hand and let him spin me around the kitchen.

I won't lie and tell you those first few months after losing Ella were not hard. We made sure to follow her advice to keep living. He did what she said, and opened the lockbox in her room. In it sat a stack of notes. She wrote down everything. A list of every question a new parent may have. Her best mom advice. We sat there for hours reading all the notes, crying our eyes out.

Here, in this kitchen, as the man of my dreams spins me while smiling down at our daughter, I thank God he got us through it all.

The doorbell rings, and he pulls me in and kisses me hard. "I'll get that."

He walks away, and I take a moment to look around the room decorated with all the butterfly decorations I could find.

"It looks amazing," Claire gushes as she walks in with Ella now tucked into her side. "Your mama did such a good job, huh? I'm gonna have to get you to help me when it's this little dude's first birthday," she says, patting her stomach.

"I still say he's coming today, and he's going to be Ella's little birthday twin," I tell her.

"I sure hope so, I'm exhausted," she says. "I was going to wait for everyone to get here, but we thought maybe it would be best to do it early," she says, handing me a bag as Layton and Tyler walk in.

"Okay?" I say, confused as she hands me Ella.

"Layton, you need to help Ella open it."

Ella takes that as her cue and rips a piece of tissue paper from the bag.

"I'm not sure she needs help." He laughs as he looks in the bag, immediately going silent before pulling a stuffed bear made of different colored patches. *All of his mom's bandanas.*

"I hope it's okay. When we were packing her stuff, I saw they were in the donation bin, and I took them."

He walks over and wraps Claire and Tyler in a huge hug. "It's perfect," he says before turning to Ella. "Look what Aunty Claire and Uncle Tyler got you, baby girl. It's a mommom bear." He says, handing the bear to her.

Ella wraps her arms tightly around the bear smiling. I set her down on her mat watching her giggle as she happily tries to eat its ear.

"I'm so glad she likes it. I've been stressing out for weeks about that bear."

"It's perfect." I reassure her.

"Seriously, Claire, it's amazing," Layton agrees.

"Look at that," Tyler says, looking down at Ella.

We all look following his eyes to her where a small butterfly sits on the nose of the bear.

I look up to the sky smiling.

"Only your mom would actually follow through on the butterfly thing," I say looking over at Layton who has the biggest smile across his face as he walks over gently letting the butterfly climb on his finger before walking to the front door letting it fly away.

"She better come back next year too—a deals a deal," he says before turning to wrap me in a hug. I know he's hiding the fact that there is a tear running down his cheek, so I pull him in and kiss it away.

"She will."

If you are in a domestic violence situation, please know you are not alone. This is the number for the DV hotline, 800-799-7233. You are amazingly strong.

Want more of Magnolia Falls Ranch
read book one, Claire and Tyler's story
Unbreak Me
Available on Amazon and signed copies on my Tik-Tok shop
C.A. Grieco Author
Keep an eye out for Luke's story coming in 2024

I have been sitting here for a while trying to find the words to even began to thank all of my readers. The truth is I don't think there is anything I can write that can put into words how incredibly grateful I am to you all.

Seven years ago, I wrote the first book in this series with a newborn baby tucked into my chest and a toddler on my lap. My husband was working crazy hours and when he'd walk through the door at 3 am, I'd read him what I wrote for the day. Finally, I said the end, and he begged me to publish. A tiny part of me thought maybe I could use my little story to better our lives, but a bigger part of me was convinced it wasn't good enough.

I let the fear win and I shoved that book in a file and didn't open it again until last year. My husband was part of a large company wide lay off and for the first time in years, it felt like we could both breathe again. That probably sounds insane, but when the man you loves works a dangerous job, you constantly wonder if it will be the last day you watch him leave. I told him I wanted to try putting my book out there. So he took the next few months and poured everything into life; homeschooling, kids, our little farm, everything thing a stay-at-home parent needs to do. I poured everything into book one.

October 3rd on my thirty-first birthday, I finally hit publish. I was terrified, but I had this tiny bit of hope this could be our answer. November 17th you guys changed not only my life but my family's life. We went into the movies for our son's birthday and when we walked out, my phone wouldn't stop going off. I had sold one-hundred copies of my debut novel on TikTok. Every single day after that for months, you guys completely sold me out. You guys changed everything.

I know to you guys it's as simple as buying a book and reading it, but to me it's everything. The fact that you took your time and money to support me and my dream is the most amazing thing in the world. So thank you all so much for reading my little stories, following my journey, and supporting me.

I hope you guys see me and realize you can have your dreams come true. A lot of the time, the person holding you back the most is yourself. Don't be like me and wait 7 years to follow your dreams.

To my husband, I can't thank you enough for everything over the last thirteen years. You have always had more faith in me than I could ever have in myself. Thank you so much for every sacrifice you made for our family. For building us this beautiful life. For giving me the chance to go after my dreams and believing in them. I know we were young without a clue in life when we fell in love, but I am so damn proud of us. I love this life we've built, and that you showed me true love is real.

To my children, I hope you guys watching me encourages you to chase all of your dreams. I hope you never let the fear of failure or judgement hold you back in life. Everything I do in this life is for you three. I love you with every single piece of me. My greatest accomplishment in life will always be you boys.

To my family, thank you for all the faith you had in me. Never in a million years did I think it would go so far, but even when you guys saw a glimpse of hope I could make it, you didn't hesitate to help. I never could be where I am without that. I'm so blessed to have such an amazing family.

To my best friend, I am so glad I have you in my life. Thank you for always being here when I need you. Thank you for believing in this chaos without a doubt. I know no matter how crazy hectic life gets, I can count on you. I am so lucky to have you as a friend.

To my editor Samantha (Samantha the spicy editor) thank you so much for all the help with my books. You know firsthand how much I need you. I truly appreciate you so much.

Made in the USA
Middletown, DE
27 May 2024